You're Welcome

By
S. M. Anker

FIRST IN THE SERIES

SAS

This is a work of light speculative fiction. Names, incidents, places, characters, events and businesses, are either the products of the author's imagination or are used strictly in a fictitious manner. Any resemblance or reference to actual persons, either living or dead, actual events, places, or businesses is entirely coincidental.

Copyright © 2013 by S. M. Anker

ISBN 978-1490389509

For my Family with Love

Joe, thank you for your patience, understanding and encouragement.

Prologue

Recently I received a box in the mail from my best friend with this note.

Sam, if you are reading this then you received Nanny's suitcase. I'm away on another adventure. In the meantime, I thought you could hang on to these for me. Sas.

I popped the latch on the suitcase. It was full of some of her notebooks. The one on top had a large number one on the front so I opened it to the first page. It read 'My Twelfth Birthday.' I'll enjoy reliving those early adventures. Perhaps you will too.

You're Welcome

Chapter One

Sas and I have been friends since we started four-year-old pre-school together. We live on the same block and became fast friends who were 'joined at the hip' her father would say. There isn't very much that I don't know about her. Her real name is Sally, but no one has ever called her that. She has always been Sas, even in school. Her grandfather on her father's side called her that when she was born, and it stuck. Her pigtails, when braided, measure exactly seventeen, and three-quarter inches at the moment. A week ago, they had been two inches longer but her mom thought they were getting too long so she cut them. She thinks the color red is the coolest, likes orange soda, plays the piano and drums, and most of all wishes she was an only child.

The house she lives in is completely different than when it was first bought. It started out a small house which had four adequately sized rooms that changed every few years as her parents continued to expand their family. She told me once that her mother bought the house one day while her father was at work. This was way before Sas's older sister Amelia was even born. Her mom paid seventy-five hundred dollars for the house sometime in the late nineteen-forties.

When you come in the backdoor there is a small hallway with one set of stairs going up and another set of concrete steps leading down into the basement. The hallway was a good place to take off wet boots and coats during the winter. It kept from dragging all the slush into the house. Sas sometimes kept her slippers in the hallway and liked that they were a little on the cold side when she put her feet into them. I have to tell you, Sas has some very peculiar behaviors.

The hallway also has a milk chute in the wall next to the back door where the milkman would leave them milk and eggs every day. He brought butter too until her

You're Welcome

father decided to drive across the state line to get margarine a few times a year. I took the long drive with them once.

Up the steps from the hallway entered into a kitchen. I guess I would call it a kitchen now, back then there was no sink. The dishes had to be done in the bathtub. The main floor doesn't sit on the ground level like other houses in the area. Her parents always thought it was safer for the house to be up higher. No one could walk up to a window and look inside.

In addition to the bathroom, there was one bedroom facing the main road. A set of cement stairs in the front of the house lead to a door that opens into a small living room.

Over the years, the family grew from three to a total of eleven. She has both older and younger brothers and sisters. I'm the youngest of three children and don't know what it feels like to be an older sister. I have always been the baby.

Sometime after Sas's oldest brothers Richard and Arthur were born her parents added a new bedroom off the kitchen for themselves. It was a good size bedroom with a bed, a chest and a long dresser all in a blonde wood finish. The closet her father built is larger than any closet I have ever seen. Not only does it have two sides to hang clothes, it has shelves across the top for added storage. I can actually walk into it and move around. Homes don't have large closets. In fact, they were very small and friends in the neighborhood wanted one when he would show it to them.

The room, however, was not heated. They didn't extend the vents into it. It was always cold except maybe in July and August. Her mother said the cold killed most of the germs and they slept better and didn't get as sick. Sometimes in the middle of winter Sas could tell the windows were even opened when she came down for breakfast because she could feel the cold even though the kitchen was heated. The original bedroom of the house was large enough until Sas started to get a bit older. A few months before her younger sister Helene was

You're Welcome

born, her father decided to add a second story to the house.

The addition took about three months and was overseen by a longtime friend who happened to be a very capable carpenter. He would come to the house prepared to have four young children running around and getting in the way. He made the days fun by wearing these very silly glasses that had eyes that would pop out on springs or he would give them matching bandanas. He also let them watch and ask hundreds of questions as he and his crew were working. As the project took shape, the house seemed to come alive. Everyone was very excited, and they finished only days before the baby came.

Over time there were six girls and three boys that occupied the three bedrooms and one bathroom that gave them their own space. All of the floors were covered in light tan carpet. It was very soft because the carpenter put something called foam underlay between the floor and the carpet itself. This helped keep the sound level down. At the time it was built, eight feet prancing around made an awful lot of noise and that only got worse as the years continued. It was much nicer to walk on then the tile floors downstairs.

The children played on the tiles before the upstairs was built. Each of the squares had some type of game imprinted on it. One was a checkered board, and another was set up for playing a game of Tiddlywinks. When the new staircase was built, leading to the addition, it covered most of the old floor, but she could get to it from the closet under the stairs and Sas liked sitting under the stairs when I came over. It was one place that we could be by ourselves. They called it the 'little room.'

One of the cool things in the little room was the clothes chute. The kids no longer had to take their dirty clothes all the way down to the basement. They could throw them down the chute and their mother could open the chute in the basement and get the clothes out.

The best thing about the new addition was that her parent's bedroom was

You're Welcome

downstairs and they rarely ever went up there. Their mother had taught them all to clean their own rooms and expected it to be done every Saturday morning.

Eventually, her three brothers shared one room. It was a large square that did not have a closet. Their closet is across the hallway and it is gigantic. Her father is so smart for insisting on making the closets so big. My closet is only about one fifth the size. Like Sas's room, their room is furnished with two sets of oak wood finished bunk beds and two dressers.

The other two bedrooms also have good sized closets with two hanging bars for clothes and a shelf to store things. Amelia, Sas, Helene, and Victoria shared the biggest room later when Margaret, Victoria, and Ellen moved from the bedroom on the first floor to the upstairs.

Their mom decided it would be a good idea to separate the twins for sleeping. Margaret and Victoria cried and complained about it for at least two months. Of the two, Margaret had a quieter personality so her dad decided she would be the one to sleep with Ellen in the third bedroom which was the smallest. It had a double bed and dresser. It faced the main road on the other side of the house looking out towards the old Falls Tavern, whose roof blew off in a bad storm. We told everyone it was a tornado because we were not sure if it was or not. Everyone in town was waiting to see if they would tear it down and rebuild or sell the land.

All of the bedrooms upstairs had these sideways windows. There were two in each room. Instead of opening by lifting the window up, you had to push it to the side. They were easy to open and close, but you had to stand on the bed to look out of them. They were the right size to set a box fan in during the summer when it got hot. Anyone with an upper bunk could look out the window and it was great sleeping with the windows open.

I only slept over a few times. To say that Sas stayed at my house for sleepovers most of the time was an understatement. You might say it was her second home.

You're Welcome

Sas liked getting away from all the commotion at her house and her mom seemed to understand that.

Next to the smaller bedroom was a bathroom. Small for a bathroom that was being used by nine children and fairly basic. The room was painted pale yellow with a sink, toilet, and bathtub. About half way up the wall around the tub were yellow tiles with a row of gray tiles around the top. The fixtures were all shiny silver including the toilet paper holder and towel rack.

There were always yellow flowered towels and washcloths hanging on the rack but they were there for decoration. A cart in the hallway kept a steady supply of towels and washcloths that they could use on a daily basis. Sas always hung her wet towels over the closet door in her bedroom. The other kids let them dry over the tub. Amelia was very artistic. Sas told me once that she would definitely be famous someday or at least have a good career. Last year she was on a Fun Film kick and made these pretty balls for all over the house. There was a yellow one hanging in the corner of the bathroom. It was just something else for Sas to dust.

It was a great house if you didn't count the bathroom. Sas's dad realized that when she was around six so he put a new toilet in the basement for them to use when they came inside from playing or if someone was in the one upstairs. It was built in the space under the steps leading into the kitchen. Under the stairs has always been creepy. We dared each other to crawl under there and around the corner into this very dark space. Her dad sometimes kept fermenting wine jugs there along with half empty cans of paint from some project he was working on.

I don't know when it happened but not long after the bathroom was built one of the glass panes in the door broke and if you looked at it you could either see the silhouette of an Indian or that of Abraham Lincoln. He liked the way it looked and never did fix it.

You're Welcome

The basement also had two large utility tubs that Sas loved washing her hair in. It was hard to get all of it rinsed it the tub upstairs and she found it much easier. There was a room where the heating oil was stored in a large tank and they would fill the tank with a long hose through the window in that room.

The fruit cellar was on the basement wall at the front of the house. Her mother kept canned vegetables and fruits there. She got most of their food from her own garden and orchard. On the opposite wall there was an opening about three feet long and one foot high. If you looked inside the opening with a flashlight all you saw was dirt. It is the space under her parents' bedroom. Her father also has a work bench down there and it is where the ironing board is kept. Sas loves to iron clothes and it is always cooler in the basement during the summer because of the cement brick walls.

Sometime after the twins and Ellen moved upstairs, the original bedroom and living room were made into a much needed larger living room and the doorway between the living room and kitchen was moved. They purchased new furniture for the room and got a television.

A few years later when her father had the downstairs kitchen remodeled, he put the old kitchen counter cabinet in Sas's room for them to use for their clothes and as a desk for doing homework. It made a very cool dresser. When you opened the silverware drawer you found socks. The larger doors when opened revealed a huge space to stack tops and pants and shorts. If you pulled on the shelf it slid out so they could get to the stuff easily. How many friends do you know with a kitchen cabinet in their bedroom? Later when they got bigger dressers they used the cabinet for toys and other stuff.

Then there was the outside space. The yard was a child's dream. There was a house on the side closest to the main road. Three children lived there and they had a very old brick fireplace at the back of their property. On the other side of that house, closest to the main road, was a paved

You're Welcome

parking lot and after a few years the owners of the Falls Tavern finally sold their property to some cousins and they opened a new burger joint called the Water Fall on the same corner. This was the best thing that happened to our little corner of the world. Sas could see it from the upstairs bathroom window and watched the older kids gather there after football games.

The main part of the backyard was enormous. Enough room for flowerbeds, a large garden and planted evergreens that looked like Christmas trees. Her father built a cement patio, a steel pipe swing set, and a clothes line. It had a very large chestnut tree near the back of the yard which was great for climbing. The tree didn't actually belong to them; it hung over from the neighbor's yard and her mom thought it was dangerous. Sas's bedroom window looked out onto that property. It wasn't a single family home like hers; it was a three story flat. A young family lived in the top flat and Sas could see right into their kitchen window if she looked at it from the top bunk when it was her turn to sleep up there.

Behind the backyard was an orchard. It was filled with apple, cherry, pear, and peach trees. The orchard also had vines of white grapes that her father used when he made wine. Beyond the orchard was an open field that was being developed into a shopping center. There would be about thirteen shops including a barbershop, and sweet shop. The local paper said it would also have a department store, pharmacy, hardware store and a grocery store. So how perfect was that?

After the building started and the concrete was poured, it was a great place to roller skate, especially in front of the shoe store when it was finished. The store front had these huge windows that formed a U-shaped display. The floor in the space had little tiles and when you rode your skates over its sidewalk you could hear the clink, clink of the skates going over the grooves. The parking lot took up the rest of the space so when you walked out the

You're Welcome

gate from the orchard it felt like you were leaving paradise for downtown.

During the summer when the town was celebrating the Bake your Apple Festival they would have a big carnival set up on that parking lot with food, games and rides. Sas's favorite was the Tilt-a-whirl.

Chapter Two

I talked to her the night before it happened. The night they went to Packard Mills which was in another shopping center about fifteen miles west. Sas loved going shopping there with the family. It was one of those adventures that happened maybe four times a year. It took planning to get that many people ready, in the car and out the door.

They made a stop first at the Schuster's store to look for winter coats. It was across the street from the Lake Drive Outdoor Movie Theatre and because it was almost Halloween and the nights came earlier, there was a movie already playing when they got there. She watched as much as she could until her older brother grabbed her by the hand and she pulled it away saying "Thanks for nothing Richard." "You're welcome," was always his response. That night she heard him give this weird little giggle afterwards. It would have turned into a full-fledged

You're Welcome

sibling fight but her parents called out to hurry up and that was that, no more movie.

There were several reasons she liked getting out to Packard Mills. One was her mother would let her go looking on her own as long as she didn't go very far. She would pretend that she was an only child there to pick out all new clothes for school. Not that she was unhappy with her wardrobe at home. Her mother was an excellent seamstress and didn't work outside of the home and had the time to sew when she wasn't taking care of the house and all of her children. Most of Sas's clothes were not store bought. She would get clothes passed down from Amelia and then she would pass down things to her younger sisters. Sometimes she wished that she would grow taller than her big sister so she could pass something down to her for a change. Today she pretended. She held up clothes in front of herself and looked in the long mirrors scattered around the girls department to see exactly how they looked. Usually before she wanted it to, the fun came to an end and it was time to go home. The other reason she liked going to Packard Mills was that on most of these excursions with the family, they usually ended up at the Dairy O ice cream parlor.

Sas's father always tried to make ice cream a bonding time. With nine kids it was a treat to go out for it. Every Sunday evening though, around seven, before the Ed Sullivan show her father would make sundaes. He would always have chopped nuts, butterscotch, fudge and caramel toppings, whipped cream and cherries for the top. This night at Dairy O, she had a chocolate and vanilla swirl in a cookie cone.

She heard her sister and brother tell their parents thank you and when her father said "You're welcome," they both giggled so much her brother Arthur lost the top of his cone. She couldn't figure out what was so funny. The thought went in and out of her brain so fast that she said she enjoyed finishing her cone.

You're Welcome

When it was time to leave there were so many that had to get into the car it was like packing a can of sardines. Everyone had their own spot. Her spot was riding on the muffler hump on the backseat floor facing the back window of the car. She said that riding backwards let her view the world from a different perspective but she once told me she didn't like the feeling of going backwards. Usually, she fell asleep on the ride home. Not that night. It was her birthday tomorrow. She would be twelve years old and she was too excited.

On that next morning her mother called everyone down for breakfast. She had finished making a large pot of Sas's favorite thing, oatmeal. Sas loved it so much she could have eaten oatmeal for breakfast every day of the week if her mother would let her. Her mom was helping her younger brother James get ready for school and told her to help herself. That was a huge mistake. She ate the entire pot and made herself so sick she couldn't go to school. So now, on her birthday, she had to stay home and when someone stayed home from school at her house there were two rules. No television and no being out of bed unless you had to use the bathroom. So up the stairs she went, she undressed, put her pajamas back on, and got back into bed.

Before her older brother Richard left for school she got up and said she had to use the bathroom but told him he could finish getting ready first. He said "Thanks sis, I'm done." as he was coming out and she said "You're welcome." as the bathroom door was closing behind her. Then she heard a faint giggle from her brother, like he was a million miles away, in the softest whisper. She said she opened the bathroom door again quickly, but he was already gone.

Back to bed she went and before long she was fast asleep. Later in the day she got up and went downstairs to see if her mother was still in the house with her littlest sister Ellen. They were gone, probably up at the shopping center. She loved these times when she was in the house all by herself. She pretended that

You're Welcome

she was the owner of the house. She poured herself a glass of milk and pretended it was coffee and ate a couple of graham crackers then she went back to bed.

She didn't wake up until it was almost time for her father to come home from work. That would be at four o'clock. You could set your watch by it. Her mother would always be there waiting for him to come in. He would give her a kiss, clean up, and within a half hour she would have food on the table. Tonight they would be having a birthday supper for Sas. Her mother always made everyone's favorite dish on their special day. Sas's was chop suey with soy sauce.

There would be a mound of cooked white rice in a bowl and the kettle with the chop suey would be placed on a hot pad in the middle of the table. She would get to serve herself first. After the fiasco with the oatmeal that morning her mother told her to be sure to leave some for the rest of the family. She took a helping of white rice and put it on her plate making a well in the middle of it with her spoon. Then she took one ladle scoop full of the chop suey and put it in the middle of the well. She always tried to make her food look pretty. Using the bottle of soy sauce for decorating, she squirted a fine line around the top of the mound of rice before mashing it all together and eating it. It was the right amount.

She didn't want to fill up because there would also be a peach pizza, her third favorite, for dessert instead of the traditional birthday cake. Sas thought her mother should sell her recipe for this delightful treat to the bakery.

It looked like a pizza but the crust was made with a sweet dough, the kind her mother used for elephant ears, which were by the way Sas's second favorite dessert. The first was bread pudding. You could never have enough favorite desserts. The pizza was layered with canned peaches that her mother made from the fruit tree in the orchard and bits of margarine and syrup. The crumble topping was thick and always baked to perfection and the

You're Welcome

perfect color brown. I had it many times and even tried to get my mom to make it but it wasn't the same. With no place to put candles on the pizza her father would stick one candle in a mound of leftover rice and light it.

Richard would turn off the kitchen light and they would all sing Happy Birthday to her while she made a wish and blew out the candle. Then the lights would go back on and someone would always try to get her to tell her wish, but she never would tell. If you told your wish it wouldn't come true.

I knew that her wish was something she had been thinking about a long time. She wished that this year she would have time to be all by herself. As I said before, it was a great place to grow up but with so many people living in one house there wasn't very much alone time.

After blowing out the candle came the presents. This year her mother and father got her, her very own radio. It was all she wanted. She had said so to me, the week before while we were playing records at

S. M. Anker

my house, "I hope my parents get me one of those small transistor radios, you know the kind with the antenna and the AM and FM channels and earphones." In addition, she also received two new beautifully embroidered pillowcases from her Nanny and cards from all of her brothers and sisters. Helene had even helped Ellen and the twins make her one.

Later they made her go through the birthday tradition of spankings on her butt and a pinch to grow an inch. She was glad that she didn't stay sick all day from the oatmeal that morning. It could have ruined her entire day. After supper was over and the taste of her second piece of peach pizza was lingering on the tip of her tongue, she watched some television. Normally it would be her turn to do dishes, but because it was her birthday, her younger sister Victoria had to dry them after Helene washed. One other thing, her birthday happened to be on a Friday that year and it was also homecoming weekend at the high school. That meant that later after the game she

You're Welcome

could watch all the kids that were up at the Water Fall out of the bathroom window. That would be such a good ending to her special day.

She told me that around nine o'clock she decided to go upstairs. Richard had taken Arthur with him and was out with some friends but would be back at curfew and Amelia was busy practicing her Hawaiian guitar lesson. The younger kids were already in bed for the night so she went into the bathroom and locked the door. She didn't turn the light on because it was easier to see out the window with it off. There were enough lights outside the window so that she could still see very well inside the bathroom.

She unlocked the window. It wasn't like the bedroom windows. It was very large and she had to lift it up to open it. The toilet was right next to the window so you could kneel on the seat and see out of it. Once the window was open you had to also lift the storm window but there would be no screen on it. It was a bit chilly out that night. Autumn had already come to the area. The trees had already turned outrageous shades of reds, oranges and yellows. Sas decided to go back to her bedroom and get her housecoat before she let the cold weather in. She got it from her Nanny for Christmas last year. It was made of the softest material and she let me wear it sometimes. It was peach colored with four inch wide stripes of cream running on either side of the zipper that went from the bottom all the way to her chin. It also had two large front pockets which were wonderful for keeping things in.

I couldn't do justice to what she told me happened after she got her housecoat on and since I have her notebooks, I'll let Sas tell you in her own words.

You're Welcome

Chapter Three

Quite warm now in my housecoat, I lifted the storm window and tried to listen to what was being said by the teenagers who were outside eating their hamburgers and fries. I could stand there watching for hours and hours but tonight some of them came over with Richard and Arthur and they all sang Happy Birthday to me. I was very moved by this out-of-character gesture by my big brothers. I yelled to them "Thank You." and before I could bat an eyelash they were gone, but I heard their faint giggle and found myself giving what should have been my brother's response, "You're welcome."

I don't know what came over me but I felt like I was falling. All the yellow tiles that were on the walls above the tub were moving around and around making me dizzy. The gray tiles were now blending with them. I felt so sick that I lifted the toilet seat because I thought I was going to puke. I tried, but it wasn't going to happen. After a while my head stopped spinning but the nausea in my stomach was overwhelming. I stood up to look out at the Water Fall again, but I couldn't see it. It wasn't there. I couldn't see the house next door either. Everywhere I looked all I could see was black. There were no street lights or planes that sometimes flew over the house at that time of night and I couldn't even see the stars in the sky. The bathroom itself was very dim now.

About ten minutes went by and I splashed some cold water on my face to make sure I was awake and not dreaming. I even pinched my arm and then screamed I pinched myself so hard. I was awake and I was in my bathroom, however, beyond that I was not sure what was happening. I didn't turn the light on but knew there was a flashlight in the medicine chest above the sink. Daddy had put it there when the bathroom was first built in case we ever lost power and needed it. I opened the door and felt until I found it. After turning it on I shined it out the window. Nothing, still only

You're Welcome

blackness. I blinked my eyes, but I couldn't even see the shopping area parking lot. After what seemed like an eternity, but was actually about a half hour, the gray tiles from the wall started moving again, realigning themselves from the wall to the floor, over the toilet and right up to the window.

The first tile seemed to be glowing and pulsating on the floor as if to beckon me to step on it. I didn't want to do that so I stood there waiting for all of it to end. It didn't. After a while I tested that first tile to see if it could hold my weight. The tile was only two inches by five inches but when I stepped on it, it felt solid under my foot. Solid as if it was one of the full size concrete steps leading to the basement. I took the next step carefully, holding very tight to the side of the window. I thought that was as far as I would be able to go. I was fairly tall already and if I walked up any farther I would slam right into the window. When I had taken the second step though, it didn't feel like that so I took the third, and then the fourth. I

S. M. Anker

looked around and everything in the room looked like it was the same size. I felt and looked like I was also the same size. How was that possible? I was standing on the last tile and right out of nowhere another one appeared and so step after step, I kept walking, right out the bathroom window.

I should have felt the cold of the night and the wind through my housecoat but I was very comfortable. As I was on the second floor of our house, I also expected to fall flat on my face. Once outside the window the tiles continued to appear and I walked as if it was a set of stairs. I walked right down into where Mom's special flowerbed should be. Since I couldn't see it I had to be very careful not to damage any of the flowers. She planted it from seeds that were sent to her by her closest friend. She was a ballerina who had moved away. She sent Mom seeds or clippings from every city she played and Mom cherished each and every flower in it. I looked around and the most peculiar thing happened. I started to see things again. The flowerbed was there and everything looked okay. As much as I was excited to see what was going to happen, I didn't want to ruin Mom's flowers.

The house next door was back as well as the Water Fall. However, when I finally walked over to talk to some of the kids, no one could hear me. No one could see me. I could interact with them but it didn't change anything they did. I took off the hat of one of the boys talking to Richard and I had it in my hand, but seconds later the boy took his hat off and put it on the girl standing next to him. I had his hat still in my hand. How could that be? I threw the hat in the trash bin.

I looked back at my house and could see the light on in the small bedroom. One of my little sisters had to be up. Then I saw the bathroom light go on and could see Margaret standing in the window looking out. The window wasn't open. Then the light was out and so was the light in her bedroom. She must have gone back to bed. I didn't even know if anyone knew I had left. In that moment I didn't care. I figured I was having the dream of all dreams and would wake up in the morning like usual. I didn't know how to get back so I decided to see what it was like being out past curfew.

At that point I wondered if I could actually get something to eat. I walked up to the counter and ordered a cheeseburger and small fry, but no one could see or hear me so when I heard someone else order the same thing and it was placed in a bag on the counter, I picked up the bag to see what would happen. The guy who ordered the food was taking his bag off the counter and he walked out the other door. The bag I had was real, it had real food inside. It was hot, so I sat down on the built in bench along the side of the building and ate it then took the bag off my lap and threw it away. I found I was thirsty afterwards and went back inside until I heard someone order a chocolate shake and grabbed it as soon as the clerk set it down. Again, I watched a man take the same shake and hand it to his daughter. The shake I had was cold, and it tasted the same as usual. Again I

You're Welcome

noticed that when I took it no one else could see it. So how is it that I was able to interact with these people and the food and nothing in their world was changed? I should have been more concerned about what was happening but then I noticed that people were starting to leave and the front clerks were cleaning up and I guessed they were getting ready to close.

I heard a few of the older girls say that they were headed to the big park along the lake road so I decided to go with them. I wasn't sure how that would work but when the car door opened, I climbed in. There were three girls in the front seat and three girls and a boy in the back seat. One of the girls was me and we were not squished at all, so off to the park we went. We played on the swings and teeter totters and hung out. I had to use the bathroom so I walked away from the group. When I came out, the car and kids were gone. I thought, now what? It didn't take long to figure out that I was by myself if I wanted to be. Had my wish come true?

I could do anything. The ranger's office was next to the bathrooms so I went there and hung out until someone opened the door and I was able to slip inside. I never tried opening the door myself but thought if I got a similar opportunity in the future to try it, I should.

I had never had coffee before. Mom would never have let me have it so I had a donut and I tried a cup of coffee. I can't say I liked it. Afterwards I decided to wander around the park to see what it was like at night. The park always closed at dusk so I had never been there this late. I have to say it was a bit spooky. I heard all kinds of noise; some of it frightened me but not enough to go back.

I saw so many people in a park that is supposed to be closed. Some sleeping under benches, one was swinging on the swings in another part of the park and others were playing cards. I walked over to them and picked a few aces out of their hands and set them down on top of the

You're Welcome

deck then sat and watched as two of them ended up with three-of-a-kind hands with three aces each. This would make a good episode of the Twilight Zone.

Some part of me told me that I should be scared, but I wasn't. It was so nice to be out alone. Then it dawned on me, and I hadn't thought about it in a while because most of the time I don't get a chance to get away from my family, but Mom always says that if you ever find yourself alone, you're not because God is always with you. Did I want to wish he wasn't there?

I walked back to the ranger's station and walked in behind a second officer. It must have been getting colder out because he walked in complaining about the frost on the ground and turned up the heat. I was still very comfortable with my housecoat and then I realized I didn't have any shoes on. I had been walking around on the ground barefoot. Come to think of it, some of the people in the park didn't have shoes either. I bet their feet were cold.

S. M. Anker

It was getting very late and I still had to figure out how to get back home. A short time passed and I heard one of the officers say he was headed to make rounds then get a BBQ sandwich and he asked the other guy if he wanted one. "No, but bring me back a root beer float." It turns out the drive-through is open later than the counter is. Before we went out the officer went into a small refrigerator and took out what looked like wrapped sandwiches and put them in a bag.

This time I got to take a ride in a truck. He had opened the door on the passenger side to lay the bag on the seat, and I jumped in before he closed the door. The radio was playing some rock and roll song that I happened to know so I started singing and then clear out of the blue he starts singing and we were doing a duet and the harmonies were outstanding. At least on my side of where ever I was it sounded good. What fun I had. What a great twelfth birthday. We started riding around the park and every once in a while

You're Welcome

he would stop and grab the bag and walk over to one of the people still in the park and ask if they would like something to eat. If they said yes, he would hand them one of the wrapped sandwiches from the bag. If they said no, he laid one close and said, "For later then." When the bag was empty we headed out of the park. The closer we got to my house the more I realized that I shouldn't be out with total strangers and wondered how I was going to get back to my bedroom.

When we arrived, I decided to try to get out of the truck myself. I hoped it would work. When he stopped by the window to give his order he didn't even notice that the passenger side of the car had opened and closed. I walked up alongside of the window where he would get his food and when the clerk handed him the bag; I slipped my hand in, took it, and left. He also got a bag and drove away. I ate the sandwich and finished the float as I headed across the parking lot. I walked over the neighbor's front lawn and back to my house. There were no tiles pulsating outside to walk back upstairs. The back door would be locked but as I got to the door I noticed it was pulsating. I also saw Richard was walking up the backyard from the shopping center direction with Arthur. He put a key in the lock, opened the door and I walked in with them. I walked up the stairs and into my bedroom. Victoria was awake reading. I walked over to get into bed, but to my surprise I was already there. I was so tired at this point that trying to figure out what was happening was going to have to wait. I crawled into bed and didn't even disturb myself and fell fast asleep.

Chapter Four

The day after my birthday, I woke up early and got out of bed. I saw myself still sleeping. I went into the bathroom. As soon as I closed the door the tiles started glowing and pulsating. A single tile moved away from the wall towards the floor and I stepped on it. Immediately the tiles looked fine and stopped glowing. There was no school, so I waited to see what the day would bring. It appeared everything was back to normal as there was only one of me at breakfast and I didn't see a second me anywhere else. I can't say what happened last night but it was an adventure I would definitely have to share with my best friend Marley.

I was a bit afraid to say anything to her at all but it turned out to be an easy conversation. I was very surprised that she believed every word of it. I didn't have to convince her at all. I am not so sure I would have believed her if the situation was reversed. I had no reason to believe it would, but we devised a plan in case it happened again. She had a key to her house so she had another one made at the hardware store. She gave it to me. If this thing ever happened again I was supposed to go to her house and let myself in and take all her clothes out of her closet. So with a plan in place, I went about my life.

I was twelve now and in seventh grade. Day after day came and went and nothing happened. After two weeks I didn't think about it very often and soon afterwards, not at all.

We were playing Buttons on the kitchen table and Victoria was beating everyone. She usually did. Buttons was so much fun. Marley always said it, but I did believe my Dad was a genius. He made up the game and I thought he should sell it to those people who made Chutes and Ladders. Amelia had played a great move off mine and said "Thanks." I said "You're welcome." Amelia giggled and I heard Richard giggle from in the living room where he was watching television.

You're Welcome

Within a minute I started to feel sick. It was the same feeling as before, a month ago on my birthday. The room started spinning but I wasn't in the bathroom at the moment so there were no tiles swirling around. I noticed the kitchen door to the hallway was pulsating and had a faint glow about it. I remembered how the tiles in the bathroom pulsated and how afraid I was of stepping on that first one. I wasn't sure what the door wanted me to do so I got up out of my chair and grabbed the doorknob.

When I looked back at the table I was still sitting in the chair while the game continued. It was so strange.

No one noticed, so with my hand still on the doorknob, I turned it. The door opened and as I walked down the stairs to the back door I found myself riding down the escalator at the department store. I jumped off at the bottom and caught the going up escalator and left the store. I had been carrying the key to Marley's house so I decided I would go straight there and empty her closet out like we had planned.

S. M. Anker

I had been out earlier in the day and it was very cold but again walking, even without a coat, I felt warm and comfortable. I was also walking around in my stocking feet. Marley lived about two full blocks away on the same street as I did. When I got to the end of my part of the block the road zigzagged for about three hundred feet. I lived on what we called the 'upper' Falls Road and she lived on the 'lower' Falls Road. It only took about four minutes to get there and when I arrived her father was raking leaves in the backyard. I tried the door and it opened so I walked into the kitchen like I had done a million times before. (I made a note of this because I had been scared to try the truck door the first time). Her mother was putting the finishing touches on their supper.

I walked past her and up the stairs to Marley's bedroom. She shared it with one of her older sisters but neither of them was there. The bedroom took up the entire attic and there were two small closets. I went to her closet and took all the clothes out and put them on the bed and turned to

You're Welcome

leave. As I turned I noticed that all the clothes were back in the closet. When I grabbed them the first time they were gone from the closet. Why were they back? I grabbed them again and turned to put them on the bed and was startled because they were also still on the bed and I dropped most of them. I looked in the closet and they were still there, or at least most of them were. I grabbed everything up and took them down to the basement and threw them on top of the dirty clothes that were sorted on the floor in front of the washing machine. I had no idea how Marley would explain it to her mom but I didn't have time to figure that out. I'd talk to her later.

I wasn't ready to go home so walked back a different way that took me up towards the shoe store. As I got closer the thought came into my head that I could go anywhere I wanted and be alone for a while. It wasn't supper time yet so I decided to go for a bus ride. I waited for the city bus around the corner from the pharmacy. There wasn't anyone waiting so I wasn't sure the bus would stop to let someone out. It did though. As soon as the guy got out of the way I jumped into the stairwell of the bus. I didn't have any money with me and decided I would have to start carrying some change in the future.

I didn't feel good about not paying, but in this world it didn't seem to matter. Mom would say it was like stealing and I didn't want to do that. Last time, when I got the food I didn't pay for that either. Then I thought, what if this was some type of test all twelve-year-olds go through to see if they are being good. That would explain why Marley totally believed me. She may have been through it already and never told me. I'd have to ask her. It could also be why my older brothers and sister giggled so much. I would try to make sure that I didn't do anything that my parents would scold me for, just in case.

The bus I was on was going all the way downtown. I mean the real downtown. I had only been there once with Nanny to

You're Welcome

pick out an outfit at Gimbles. It had been a special outing a few days before she took me and Amelia to the State Fair. I got red stretch pants with little stirrups that went under the feet and a white sailor blouse with red ribbing around the sleeves and the collar and a red bowtie. I love that outfit. So, when the bus left some people off close to Gimbles I got off and started walking.

I had to cross two extremely busy intersections. The kind that had a light flashing letting me know I could walk but didn't give me nearly enough time to actually get to the other side. I got through the first one okay, but ended up running through the next one.

The windows of the store were already decorated for the Christmas season. On one hand I couldn't understand why they would do that before Thanksgiving was even over. On the other hand, I know that Mom and Dad would never make a trip downtown so this might be the only chance I would get to see them. So how could I be anything but grateful they decorated the windows early?

There were things moving in the windows. One had a choo-choo train that went through a tunnel and under and around a Christmas tree. The tree was decorated with colored lights that twinkled to the Christmas tunes that were playing on a small piano next to the tree. The window had a speaker on the outside of it so I could hear the piano music. The train would take one turn around the tree and then climb a tall mountain on the other side of the window. At the top of the window was a track that let the train circle the entire window at that level before it made its decent back through the tunnel. I watched it five or six times before I moved on to window number two. That one had a large sugar plum mountain with loads of toys all around it. There were dolls, board games, sports and art stuff, and other little things. The toys were on little platforms around the mountain and Christmas tunes were playing in that window too. Each platform was rigged so that as the music played, the toy on it would move up and down. It looked like the toys were dancing. I watched them for a while thinking something was going to fall off its platform but it didn't. I moved on to another window and memorized as much as I could. Marley would want to hear all about them. Then it dawned on me that I did remember everything that happened to me the night of my birthday so I was pretty sure I would remember this adventure too.

As I turned one of the corners to look at another window I saw there was a five dollar bill lying on the ground. That was an awful lot of money so I picked it up and asked everyone if it was theirs. I have to remember that they can't hear me. I had the bill in my hand, but there it was, still on the ground. I saw a young woman with two small children pick it up. I tried to hand her mine but again there was no connection between where I was and where she was and what she was doing.

S. M. Anker

I put the bill in my pocket and went on about the business of window looking.

The next one I loved most of all. It had white snowflakes sprayed on the inside of the window with fluffy stuff that looked like snow lying on the floor. There was an aluminum tree in the center of the window that almost filled up the entire space and this spiral light kept changing it different colors. First it was blue, then red, green, yellow and blue again. There were five life-size Christmas elves standing around the tree in the most beautiful costumes. Around and under the tree were scattered gift boxes wrapped in all different kinds of papers and bows. There were hundreds of large sparkly ornaments hung from the ceiling at random heights and every few minutes, a machine would blow the fluffy fake snow all over so that it looked like it was snowing right inside the window like a winter wonderland snow globe.

When I was finished checking out the last window I went into the store to look at everything else there was. I saved the toy department until the end. Packard Mills

You're Welcome

didn't have half the stuff I found there. I did see something I wanted to ask Santa for this year. It was a Think-a-Tron and it cost six dollars and eighty-seven cents. That is all I wanted and hoped it wasn't too much. You pick a punched card that has a bunch of multiple-choice questions that you want to have answered, feed it into the machine and then pick the answer (A, B, C, T or F) you think was correct by pushing a button. The computer then starts whirring. Lights flash and within seconds you see the right answer on a little section of tiny light bulbs. It comes with one hundred and fifty double sided cards that it can answer. There is even a little holder for each set of fifty cards and you can buy additional question packs. I bet I would be the only one on the block to have one.

After looking at everything in the store, I figured I had better see about eating something. The money I picked up was still in my pocket so I went to the restaurant across the street and stood in line until someone ordered something I liked. It only took a few minutes before someone ordered a hot chocolate and a chicken salad sandwich on a croissant. When I got my food I left the money sitting on the counter and went to find a place to sit down. That was the best I could do. I'd have to figure out how all this stuff works

Everyone was staying inside because they were cold. I wasn't cold so I was the only one eating on the patio. As I ate, I watched the people walking by. Some were in a hurry while others were strolling slowly having conversations. Others were yelling at each other and some were trying to maneuver way too many packages. I liked watching people and sat there for a very long time before I thought about going home.

You're Welcome

Chapter Five

First, I would have to find the bus stop I needed. I went back to where I got off the bus and that was a one-way street. I had to watch for a bus that was heading downtown in the same direction I had been going when I got there. After a while a bus stopped at the same stop and I jumped on thinking that at some point it would have to turn around and go back towards home. As a twelve-year-old that seemed logical to me. I didn't know about bus transfers and out of service buses yet.

That is what happened to me. I jumped on a bus and it went along for a while through the streets but drove into a terminal. There were hundreds of buses there. The bus I was on was now out of service. I followed the bus driver into a building and watched him punch some card in a machine and went into the men's room. After a while he came back out, but he wasn't wearing his uniform. He had on blue jeans and a green sweater under his winter coat. I followed him and he got into his car. I went to open the passenger side door, but it wasn't unlocked. I wondered if I could open his driver side door and crawl over him, but I was too chicken to try it. I stood there and watched him drive away.

It must have been a big shift change because about twenty bus drivers came in with their buses over the next half an hour and walked out and went to their vehicles. I saw a few women which surprised me. I thought all bus drivers were men. One of the women had to load some things in her car so the passenger side door was open, so I slipped in. There were boxes and clothes stacked on the seat, but they didn't bother me one bit. It was like they weren't there.

I had no clue where I was headed but at the very least I could go to her house and have a place to spend the night and drive to work with her the next day and catch a bus back home. I was also surprised at how fast I figured that out. I wondered, for a split second, what I was doing at home. I wanted to talk to Marley but that would have to wait for now.

When we got to the woman's house I found out she had a six-month-old baby girl and I love babies. I had four little sisters and a little brother so I had been around babies for a long time. I heard the phone ring and concluded from the conversation that the woman was talking to her mother and they made plans to have lunch tomorrow. She didn't have to go back to work for three days. I guessed it would be an interesting three days.

The woman made the baby a bottle and put her down for a nap, but she dropped her binky on the floor once and I picked it up and gave it back to her. There was no way to get around it so I left the original one there on the floor. She seemed to sense I was there but settled into a deep sleep before too long and I laid down on the floor next to her and also took a nap.

It turned out to be a very long nap. I woke up the next morning when I heard the woman changing the baby. She was still in her pajamas which reminded me that I was still in the same clothes I wore all day yesterday, but also had on twice earlier in the week.

I wondered if I could clean up. I looked around and it was the two of them in the house so when I heard her go downstairs I went into the upstairs bathroom and locked the door. I didn't know if that would keep her out because the door wasn't locked on her side of the world. It made me feel more private though. I took my clothes off and set them down on the floor. This bathroom had a shower so I opted for that because it would be quicker. I jumped in and washed my hair but when I was finished there were three bottles of shampoo.

I was reminded again that I needed to be extra careful. I also had to hang two extra towels on the towel bar. The bad

You're Welcome

part, there were at least six bars of soap. Maybe she wouldn't notice.

I washed my clothes in the sink and put the towel that I had used last around me and went into the basement to dry them. She didn't even notice the dryer was running. I also noticed there wasn't an extra set of clothes on the floor when I took them, so I figured out that if it was my stuff and I brought it with me, it would not replicate. I had to give that some thought when I got home. After I got dressed again I felt better. I did have one more extra towel to hang though.

During the first day at the house I learned her name was Barb and her husband was Bill. Their little girl's name was Jean Rae. Bill left for work before I got up so I would see him later, possibly. I knew she was going to go out for lunch but I opted to stay at the house. Barb had left the television on so I watched it most of the day and about four o'clock that afternoon Barb returned but left again a half hour later. I thought I would try to see if I could make a phone call. I didn't want to end up with two phones, so I touched the phone and then let go. There was one phone. I picked up the receiver and it was not still sitting in the phone cradle. I decided that as the phone receiver was connected to the base and I wasn't moving or lifting it that it should be safe to use it.

I dialed Marley's number. She picked up on the second ring. She usually answered the phone at her house because most of the calls that came in were for her. When she knew it was me, she said "Did you forget to tell me something."

I said "No, I had to call to tell you what was happening to me. I haven't been home in over a day."

Marley said, "What do you mean, I was talking with you only a while ago after you had your supper."

"No, we didn't." I told her. "That was the Sas that was left in your world while I left again into, I don't know what this is, my wish world." "Didn't you see the clothes I left on your bed?"

You're Welcome

"Oh, of course I did, I was putting you on." "When I saw the clothes on the bed and in the closet, I knew it had to be you." "My mom thought she was going crazy though when she saw them in the basement! I took all the extra clothes up to the Heaven on Earth thrift shop when she wasn't paying attention." "Okay, so what happened?"

I spent the next half hour or so telling her what had happened. I wasn't sure when I would get back again but that I was okay and from the sound of it, no one even knew I was gone.

We made another plan that when I did get back, if I was going to see her on the weekend I would wear my purple socks no matter what I decided to wear that day. I only wore those socks once and swore I would never wear them again because Anthony had teased me. If it wasn't until during the week I would call her and give her the code words 'purple socks' so she would know it was me. We also decided that we would call where she was the 'real world' and where I was the 'altered realm,' because it sounded cool and mysterious. We would try to think up something better later. She told me to have fun and be careful and I hung up the phone and there was still only one.

A little while later Barb and Jean Rae came back home, and she started supper. Bill came home around six o'clock and they ate at seven. I had to eat something and didn't want to leave the house. I knew if I took a plate out of the cupboard no one would notice, but there would be an extra plate when I was done. I took one anyway but found a plastic fork in the silverware drawer and would throw it away when I was finished. Barb had made a roast of beef that was so tender it melted in my mouth but still not quite as good as Mom's. I used my fork to pile what would be two serving spoons of mashed potatoes onto my plate and did the same with the corn. I managed to find the butter and a salt shaker which I threw away when I was finished using it. I ate

You're Welcome

until I felt full and put my plate in the sink with the other dirty pots and dishes.

Bill had left the television on when he came to supper so I went in and watched it. Our television at home was always turned off when we were eating supper. Mom and Dad thought that supper was the perfect time to talk as a family. If anything was going on or if anything happened during our day Dad wanted to hear about it. I usually never had anything much to add and I certainly couldn't share anything about what was happening these days.

Later when Barb was doing up the dishes I heard her ask Bill where he had found the extra plate. From the conversation they had about it, it appears she had misplaced one of the plates a week ago and she didn't know where it went. I heard Bill talking to Jean Rae later in the evening when he was changing her. He said, "Where do you suppose that plate came from Jean Rae, I know I broke it and threw it away. Maybe she is playing with me and found another one at the store." I didn't hear either of them mention it again while I was there. Managing these two separate worlds was truly a challenge.

You're Welcome

Chapter Six

On the second day, I woke up to the baby crying and screaming uncontrollably. Something was definitely wrong. I had heard my little brother James cry like that when he got colicky. That usually happened when a baby was younger though. Jean Rae might be too old for it to be that. Barb called the doctor when she couldn't make her comfortable. Oh good, I thought, another road trip. I felt bad that Jean Rae wasn't feeling well. She took another phone call a few minutes later and then Barb moved very quickly to get her dressed and into the car. I was right beside her and when her binky fell out I would put it back and occasionally throw the extra ones out the window. Barb didn't see this happening in the rear-view mirror. Barb was grateful that she wasn't screaming more. Jean Rae seemed to like me being there.

We didn't pull into a doctor's building though, we were at a hospital. I had been to a hospital a few times already. Once I went to have my tonsils out. What I remembered about that was that my dad was doing the surgery and my mom was my nurse. Mom said that didn't happen. It was the anesthesia that made me dream it. I also remembered I got to eat ice cream whenever I wanted it. The other times I went were when my little brother, the twins and Ellen were born. Today I was there because a six-month-old little girl was way sicker than I had thought. People don't go to the hospital for little things. I followed as she ran into the hospital and talked to the nurse behind the counter. She carried Jean Rae through a set of doors and I went with them. I was a bit confused for a while but after a minute I realized that we were not at the hospital because of Jean Rae.

Bill was lying on the bed. The curtains were pulled all the way around the cubicle we were in and Barb leaned over and gave him a kiss. Apparently, Bill had been at work and somehow broke his arm. He was in the process of getting a cast put on.

You're Welcome

I had a cast on my left leg once when I was three and a half. We were playing tag in the front yard and I was tackled and snap it went. The doctor said that if I had a little more meat on my bones it may not have even broke. Mom said that I didn't like having it on and Daddy took me for walks in the coaster. Once she said that I scooted out the front door, down the steps all the way to the backyard and she found me swinging on one of the swings.

Even then I liked to have adventures. Nothing has changed in nine years. Bill is the only other person I know of that had a broken bone. We were at the hospital for a few hours and when the doctor came back to recheck the cast he told him he could leave, but not to work for a few days. Then we all went in Barb's car back to their house.

Since he was going to rest the next day, Barb told him she would take the baby and go to her friend's house to work on a special project they were making for Thanksgiving. That way he would not be disturbed. She would make him some lunch and put it in the refrigerator in case he got hungry. I heard her tell him that Jean Rae had been screaming earlier in the day and that she had called the doctor. Bill asked her what the doctor said. She told him that he said to check her mouth, that she was probably teething, and she felt a little tooth coming in. Then Barb told him that is when she got the call from the hospital. Jean Rae was reluctant at first but let me feel her tooth too.

It was a relatively quiet evening after supper and Bill went to bed early. I was glad Jean Rae was okay. I watched television with Barb until she turned it off to read. I went up and laid down on the floor next to Jean Rae's crib. The baby had a few crying spells during the night, but she let me rub her back until she settled back down.

Next morning Barb kept her plans to go to her friend's house. I decided to go with her. I was completely surprised when we headed towards the South bus route. I wondered how far south we would go. We drove for a while before we got there.

You're Welcome

I spent the entire day with them. They made the most adorable centerpieces for the holiday. They were going to be used at a homeless shelter supper they were both volunteering for.

Before too long the day was over and we were headed back to Barb's house, but I was surprised when I started to recognize the area. She was headed toward my house and stopped at the fabric store. I jumped out of the car and walked past the store fronts right into the back orchard, through the backyard and when I approached the back door I noticed the milk chute door was glowing.

You have got to be kidding, is all I could think. I was going to have to go through the milk chute to get back to the real world. I opened the chute door and jumped up and crawled through the chute head first with my arms above my head. I hadn't gotten through the chute completely and was surprised when I saw Amelia sitting at the kitchen table drawing on Daddy's special paper.

She looked over her shoulder and said "Hurry, up no one is around."

I told her "Thanks." and she said, "You're welcome."

She was still giggling as I walked up the stairs to our bedroom. It wasn't my imagination then, she saw me. I hadn't completely come in through the chute yet, but she saw me. Maybe when I simply touched the knob on the chute I already switched worlds. Maybe she thought I was trying to sneak in unnoticed.

As I got ready later to go to bed I remembered I was supposed to call Marley. Her mother answered the phone so I asked to talk to her. I could hear her calling to her, up the stairs, and could also hear the thump, thump, thump of her jumping down the stairs. "Oh, hey Sas, what did you forget?" I only said, "Purple socks."

"Oh, good you're back." she said.

"First I want to know what I was doing while I was gone."

You're Welcome

Marley spent the next few hours filling me in until I heard someone breathing on the phone and it wasn't us. Marley's house phone didn't have a party line, but we did. The lady on the party line asked us to get off. Usually one would hang up the phone right away. Mom would hear about it if we didn't and that meant getting yelled at.

Today I told her I'd get off only if it was an emergency because we were working on our homework together. She said the first two times that was fine, she would try later. The third time was different. I could tell if she hung up the phone by the sound of the click when the receiver was set down. I didn't hear it, so I asked when she was going to hang up because it would take longer to get off if she didn't. Mom would have said that was being impolite. I heard the click.

I told Marley we could talk more Sunday after church before our catechism class. We were starting work on our lessons for our confirmation in one and a half years. It was supposed to be the most intense study we had to go through. We would also have to do a service project or some other form of ministry and attend at least one youth retreat. Then the week after next we would have some extra days off because Thursday was Thanksgiving and there was no school until the following Monday. I did ask her quickly about her having these adventures when she was twelve, but she said that she didn't and if she had she would have told me.

I heard her say "Night Sas." before the phone went dead. Then I heard the party line lady dialing. I didn't stay on, that would have been rude.

During the conversation with Marley, she told me that she wanted me to call her Sam now. She wasn't going to tell the other me that bit of information so she would know which one of us she was talking to if I called her Marley. We also concluded that it appeared I got a little warning about what was happening with the sick feeling and the glowing and pulsating so Sam thought it would be a

You're Welcome

good idea to put a few things together that I might need if I did leave again.

Later that night I emptied an old backpack that I used a few years ago, when I had sleepovers. I put in a bottle of shampoo, a comb, and an old towel from the back of the linen closet that Mom would never miss. I put my allowance that week and some other change I had been saving for a while into the zippered compartment. I also put in a change of clothes, pajamas, and underwear.

That's all I could think of for the time being. I hid the bag under the stairs in the little room behind the box of games that Mom kept there. I figured that it would be close enough to get to if I remembered in the moment to get it, if it happened again.

Chapter Seven

At school on the Friday before Thanksgiving no one was prepared for the day's events. We were almost finished with our second afternoon classes when the principle came on the loud speaker and told everyone to go to the gym. Once we were there, he told us that the President of the United States had been assassinated.

We were allowed to stay in the gym and talk about it with the teachers. Many children were crying and hugging each other. Some parents showed up to take their children home. I don't think it sunk into my mind what had happened until supper time and we were all talking with Mom and Dad about it. Everyone was glued to the evening news which changed from them talking about the President to news about having a new President and how he had taken his oath on board the jet. Mom said it was a very sad time for the United States and to add an extra prayer tonight for their families and our country.

Even though everyone was reeling from last week's news, Thanksgiving was a great day. I love the smell of a turkey cooking in the oven. My dad did most of the cooking on holidays. Mom made a cream cheese carrot cake for dessert this year. There were homemade dinner rolls, mashed potatoes, and corn, green Jell-O with shaved carrots, and mushroom gravy to complete the meal. It must have cost at least ten dollars to feed all of us on a holiday if I added in the cost of the B&B soda. Dad always said if you went hungry in our house, it was your own fault. There was always plenty of food and enough leftovers to eat during the week.

After supper I went and got the flashlight from the bathroom and crawled under the steps in the little room to write my letter to Santa in peace and quiet. Or so I thought. The twins saw me and Victoria kept asking what I was doing so I told them and the only way to get them to leave me alone was to help them write their letters first. I finished mine and would take them all up to the drop box at the department store.

The store was closed for the holiday, but when it reopened for business Friday it would be all decorated for Christmas. Complete with Santa's Corner where you could find all the new decorations and toys that were being offered that season. Santa would come to visit during store hours and parents would stand in line to let their children sit on his lap and tell him what they wanted. I thought I was too big for that but I still would drop off the letters. If I didn't tell him, how would he know I wanted the Think-a-Tron? I still ended up taking the four younger kids to see Santa the next day because Mom wasn't feeling well and Dad was back at work.

One outgrows that stuff soon enough, so it was fun to watch them still enjoy it. Especially James and Ellen. When they were done they all started fussing so I took them home. Sam didn't write a letter this year and all she wanted for Christmas was

You're Welcome

for her parents to remodel their basement so that she could have a party down there for her thirteenth birthday. She would be a teenager before I would.

The next few weeks went by fast. Each time I got my allowance I put some of it in the backpack when no one was looking.

It was very cold out now. Snow was on the ground and a regular section at the park had been watered and frozen over so we could go ice skating. I liked going to the park in winter to skate, although recently every time I went Mom wanted me to take one or two of the younger kids with me.

The pavilion was in the middle of the park close to the 'elephant tree.' It was shaped with large elephant trunk like limbs that were fairly close to the ground and easy to climb. We liked to hang out in it when we weren't on the skating rink. There were bathrooms in the pavilion and cubbies to put my shoes and boots in when I put my skates on.

When I walked out of the pavilion there was a walkway that was also frozen over so I could skate all the way down to the rink. All the kids in the neighborhood skated there. It was always good fun. Even if it snowed they would clean the rink and plow the snow around the outside of the rink to enclose it. This kept the area warmer as it blocked most of the cold wind. Once enough bodies got on the rink it was pretty comfortable. I could stay on it for hours. That is if I didn't have one or another sister or brother asking to go to the bathroom all the time. I found myself hoping more and more for another visit to the altered realm.

You're Welcome

Chapter Eight

I spent most of my free time, in December, skating at the park. Between homework and chores, the days flew by. One day on the way home from the park a thought came into my mind. When I came in the milk chute to get in the last time I came home, Amelia had spoken to me. She said to hurry up that no one was looking. How did she see me? Had I come back in the real world the instant I started through the chute? Was she in the altered realm? I had way too many questions and not enough answers. I'd have to ask her about it.

Before I knew it we were celebrating my little brother James's birthday. His favorite supper was a cheeseburger, fry and shake so Mom didn't have to cook anything. Daddy would get an order from each of us and usually sent me and Helene because it was usually too much for one of us to carry. He also knew that we were the only ones that didn't snitch fries on the way home. Mom made him a red velvet birthday cake with Bavarian cream filling inside. She decorated it to look like Superman flying next to a tall building. I made him a birthday card that also had him drawn on the front. I wrote, "Not a train or plane?" on the outside and inside I wrote, "No it's a birthday for James!" It was corny, but the best I could come up with.

Mom and Dad got him this large wooden construction truck. He loved it. Mom said there would be no end to what his imagination came up with to use it for. The truck made a very loud roaring engine sound and there were two small figures in the cab that bounced up and down when the truck was pulled. He could fill up the truck bed with whatever he chose to haul around. After James got his last pinch to grow an inch there was only some silverware to wash since Mom used paper plates to serve the cake.

Christmas was a few days away and I realized that it was closing in on the time when I might get to go on another adventure, but it hadn't happened yet. I

You're Welcome

found myself hoping it wouldn't come until after Christmas if it was going to happen at all. I want to be the one that opens my presents and celebrates Jesus' birth at church. I didn't care if I was there with the family for Christmas supper.

Christmas morning, I was there to sneak downstairs and look at the presents underneath the tree. Mom and Dad didn't wait too long to get up and supervise the opening of gifts. We had started a tradition a few years before of each one of us opening a present at the same time then showing what we got. I remembered how big the box was for the Think-a-Tron, so I opened the one I thought it was first. I was right. Richard was eager to see how it worked but that would have to wait until later. Next, we gave our parents the gifts we made for them. Then we exchanged the small gifts we got for each other. When that was done we opened the rest of our own gifts. I also got this cool game called Magnetel.

It was a small pool table with plastic pockets and a slick, green surface. I had to use these little magnetized disks, in a number of the games. There were nine magnetized areas on the board and the first game I learned was shuffleboard. The non-magnetized plastic disks were colored and numbered like pool balls. They slid across the surface when hit with the spring-loaded cue sticks that came with it. I got some new slippers, two new pillowcases, a sweater, and Nanny had crocheted me a new scarf.

After the presents were opened we got ready for church. On the way home, we stopped by the bakery to get soft rolls and hot shaved baked ham for breakfast. It was my favorite Sunday breakfast. If I put margarine on the bun and then put the hot ham in, it would melt the margarine and was so yummy. After breakfast I showed Richard how the Think-a-Tron worked, and we played with it for a long time. Daddy was busy making Christmas supper and Mom was finishing up with all the other little things. She had spent most of the day before baking pies. One was

You're Welcome

apple, another cherry and the last was a rhubarb pie.

We didn't have supper until after six and I had to stop playing. By the end of the day the game I played most involved stacking the magnetic disks on top of each other, on top of one of the magnetic spots on the board. Then I would take turns with Richard shooting another disk at the bottom of the stack using the cue stick, to see if either of us could dislodge the bottom disk without knocking the stack over. Richard won way more than I did. All in all, it was a good Christmas.

I got to spend a great deal of time with Sam since school was out until after the New Year. One of the things she got from her parents was a little card that said that they were going to finish off the basement during the spring and it would be ready for her to have a party for her birthday. She was so excited because they told her she could pick out some of the colors. She got some new records and a portable record player and some new clothes. We spent lots of time skating at the park and shoveling snow.

In the winter I could always make some extra money shoveling for some of the older neighbors who found the task too much for them. The shopping center parking lot had so many mountains from plowing that we went with our saucer sleds down the hills after the stores were closed. That way we didn't have to worry about cars driving into us or I should say us slamming into cars driving by.

As we were walking one day towards my backyard Sam was saying that she was going to head home the back way and thanked me for a great day of fun, I said "You're welcome." and instantly felt sick.

The gate to the back orchard was pulsating and in a second I thought; go get your backpack. I forgot completely about Sam and ran through the gate not thinking and then saw the neighbor's fireplace glowing. I decided to go in my house first. I wasn't sure if I was in the altered realm yet or not.

You're Welcome

I walked up the stairs and no one was in the kitchen so it was easy to go to the little room and grab the backpack I had repacked over a month ago, this time adding some silverware. I also ran back upstairs and took my pillow. I liked having it with me when I did any traveling and I didn't have it when I spent time at Barb's house last month. I went to the linen closet and grabbed a few pillowcases and put them on. Since I didn't know how long I might be gone that would have to do. When one case was used, I could peel off the top pillowcase and a new one was there.

I knew I didn't need my coat, gloves, or boots so I put those away in the little room and went outside. The fireplace next door was still glowing so I thought I hadn't left the real world yet but I wasn't cold. I ran around to the fireplace and touched it. It felt as if the fireplace sucked me up through the chimney, took me on a wild ride, and then spit me out.

I saw Sam leaving the area and went over to the gate where she left a note on the post next to the latch. 'I know you are off again, because when I thanked you for the great fun, you said, "You're welcome, see you tomorrow Marley." Have lots of fun. She signed it Sam. So I must have gone into the altered realm as soon as I walked through the gate but had to go through the fireplace to finish. It had to do something with the pulsating and glowing. I hadn't given any thought to what I might want to do next.

The other two adventures happened by circumstance from something I started, so if I stood there, I guessed nothing would happen. I ended up going back into the house acting like everything was normal. It was a little unsettling to see myself walking around the house and doing stuff. It paid off though. I did check, and my backpack was still under the staircase and my pillow was still on my bed. I'd have to leave them somewhere before I came back.

Later the next day I got a telephone call from Sam and heard my end of the conversation. It appeared that Sam was going to go to visit some relatives in

You're Welcome

Minnesota the next day and her mom said I could go with them. My other me asked Mom if she could go and Mom reminded her about the plans they had made to go to my grandmothers. I heard myself tell Sam that she couldn't go this time. I had gone with them once before and had a blast. So I was out of there.

S. M. Anker

Chapter Nine

I walked over to Sam's house and waited up in her room. I heard her come upstairs with her sister. They were going to bed early for the trip in the morning. Somehow, I had to let Sam know that I was there. I needed to find something small to replicate but something she would see. What could I take? If it was small, it would be easy to get rid of. She was sitting up with her legs hanging off the side of the bed. Then I saw them, two pieces of M&M candy lying on the top of her nightstand.

I picked one up and then set it down. She didn't notice. As I went to do it again, she picked up a piece and ate it and there were two left. I quickly picked one up and set it down. She noticed. She took two away and left one. I picked it up and set it down. She whispered "Sas is that you?" because her sister was on the other side of the room. I picked another candy up and set it down. "Oh it is you, I have to stop thinking I'm going crazy." "You got my note then?" I set another piece of candy down.

I then thought I had to do something else, but she thought of it first. She got up and got a notepad of paper with a pencil attached to it with a braided piece of rope. She said I should be able to write without making a second pencil if I didn't lift the pad of paper. I wrote that I overheard her conversation about the trip in the morning and asked, if it was okay, I'd like to go anyway. She said out loud, "Great."

"Great, what is great?" her sister had heard her. I wrote asking if she could see my backpack and she said "no," so I wrote that everything would be fine. She told me to sleep on the same side of the bed I used when I slept over and that she would pack a few extra clothes for me because one extra outfit might not be enough. I fluffed my pillow and then I realized that if I had my pillow and Sam couldn't see my backpack then I got them before I entered the altered realm which I probably did when I touched the fireplace. If I was right, it also meant that I wouldn't have it to sleep with in the real world. I would be going crazy looking for it. I was going to have to wait to take at least my pillow next time until after I knew for sure I was in the altered realm if I could. It all was giving me a headache and yet I was asleep before Sam could say goodnight.

Next morning came quickly and I had slept well. Before we had gone to bed the night before we decided that I would hang out and do what I needed to do and once we got to her Aunt Marie's house we would figure out how to communicate better. I was famished and could smell breakfast cooking downstairs. Sam made sure I had time to take a shower by locking us in the bathroom for a while. She talked for a long time because she knew I could hear her. I used my own shampoo and comb which worked out nicely. When I was ready I dropped my shampoo bottle on the floor, but she didn't see it. I took the piece of candy I had in my pocket and set it down on the counter. "You finished then?"

You're Welcome

Next stop breakfast. Sam put out a paper plate for me to use and I had my silverware. Once I took the plate and filled it I went into the living room to eat while everyone else ate at the kitchen table. It was going to be a brilliant week. After breakfast I threw my paper plate in the garbage. I went into the bathroom when Sam did and washed my fork off and dried it with some toilet paper which I threw into the toilet and flushed. Our trip would now begin. Sam's father got everything loaded in the car and I threw my backpack into the trunk as he was closing it. I sat on top of Sam's sister in the car and she had no clue I was there. I had plenty of room for myself and probably could have laid down across all of them and taken a nap. I didn't though.

We were headed up to Red Wing, Minnesota. It was a small historical town near the Mississippi River on Highway Sixty-one. I had gone there before, and Sam's Uncle Francis's house was right on the river. It was during the summer though and we went to a wonderful

S. M. Anker

Fourth of July picnic in Levee Park. They had a parade down the main street and the park was right on the bank of the river and I could see the main bridge in the background. They shot the fireworks from a barge on the river over the water and they lit up the entire sky. I'll never forget it. The town itself had many old buildings that dated back to the Eighteen-sixties and was the first place I got interested in looking at architecture. My father wore Red Wing steel toed shoes to work every day, so I had been excited to see where they were made. This trip was for visiting Sam's family and celebrating a late Christmas with them.

It took about seven hours to get there. We stopped for lunch around one o'clock in La Crosse which was right near the Minnesota boarder, at a restaurant called the Peddlers Palace. It had good food and had been there since the early Nineteen Hundreds. I took what was on Sam's plate to eat. She had ordered a double thick cheeseburger with pickles and mayo, and onion rings. She must have known I

You're Welcome

would be eating what she did and ordered the onion rings for me. I know she would have preferred French fries. I'll have to tell her that she should order what she wants next time that I'll be okay. Although I couldn't feel the cold temperatures outside, I certainly felt hunger in this altered realm. I was glad when she ordered a refill on her cherry cola. It was about four o'clock when we pulled into the driveway of her Aunt Marie and Uncle Francis's house.

It was already getting dark when we arrived. There was so much untouched snow and it was so beautiful. I would have to tell Sam to take some pictures. I wondered if I stood in the picture with her if I would show up.

The river was frozen over and the next day the men would be going ice fishing. I loved to fish. My father took me bass and trout fishing with him once in a while, but what I loved was ice fishing. I thought about going with them to make sure we would have enough for supper. I got this

S. M. Anker

picture in my mind of the disciple helping Jesus feed all those people. What if he was on his very own adventure in an altered realm replicating the fish and bread that day? Okay, God, I probably shouldn't have thought that. Sorry.

I would have to wait to see what happened. I grabbed my backpack when the trunk opened and followed Sam into the house. I knew which bedroom we had used last time but this time it was different. They had built an addition to the house and had two large rooms built into the former attic. Our bedroom for the week was upstairs like at Sam's house back home. Her sisters used the guest room on the first floor which meant that Sam's parents would be in the other room upstairs. After seeing the space, it was perfect. There was a hallway between the two rooms and that would give us our privacy. We were going to celebrate Christmas all over again in a couple of days when the rest of the family would come for supper and exchange gifts. What a blast, two Christmases.

You're Welcome

When the day was over we went up to bed. I took out my pajamas and put them on and laid out a change of clothes for tomorrow. Sam and I stayed up a long time after that. She had brought her notepad and pencil on the rope. I wrote, and she spoke for a few hours figuring out how she would know where I was. I thought if I had some string I could tie myself to her button hole or something and she might feel me pull on her clothes, but when we tried it, it didn't work. Everything short of the writing pad did not work. In the end we decided it would be best to talk at night like this. She would go about her day as if I wasn't there, only knowing I was. I could always replicate something if I wanted to get her attention and she would look out for it.

In the morning after breakfast the men did go fishing but the rest of us got in the car and headed out. Sam asked where we were going because she had to put on a dress and her black patent leather shoes. Her Aunt Marie only said, "You'll see."

S. M. Anker

So, it was going to be a surprise. Sam and I love surprises. We got on the interstate, so I guessed we were going far. We were also going north.

Sam kept guessing and her Aunt would say, "No, wait and see, you'll like it." Along the way I saw a highway sign that said we were headed towards St. Paul. After about an hour we got off the freeway and drove to a parking lot across the street from the Old Avalon Square Theatre.

The marquee said The Nutcracker was playing. We were going to see the Nutcracker. I had heard about the Nutcracker being in New York, but I was going to see it here in St. Paul, right now. How very exciting. I was mesmerized during the entire play. I was so hoping that I would be able to remember this experience with Sam. I hoped she would remember me being there with her. I also found myself wishing I could share this with my sisters.
'Where on earth did that come from'?

You're Welcome

My favorite parts were the Dance of the Sugar Plum Fairy and the Chinese tea performers. Maybe next year I would dress up like the Sugar Plum Fairy for Halloween. I'd ask Sam later what she liked best.

The play took about two- and three-quarter hours but it went by so fast I was surprised it was over. Once during the play, I went to the bathroom when Sam's mom went. I am getting accustomed to no one being able to see me. After the play we went to a nearby Woolworths for ice cream. Sam ordered a banana split with extra hot fudge and nuts. We both liked ours the same way.

Back home during the summer our Woolworths would have balloon days. I would pick a balloon and pop it and inside it said how much I would have to pay for my banana split. Sometimes I would get a free one and Sam would get hers for seventy-five cents and we would divide the cost between us.

S. M. Anker

I put some of the change I brought on the table. I wasn't sure if Sam could see it, but I felt better at least trying to pay for it. Afterwards the adults wanted to go window shopping so that is what we did. Sam asked her mom if she could go across the street to the park and her mom said "Okay." There were lots of families eating ice cream cones in the park and I could tell by the way they were dressed that they had been at the play too. Some of the girls had little red fur jackets and little white muffs to warm their hands in. Some of the young boys were dressed in suits that made them look like my dad when we went to church.

Within a few minutes of reaching the park something very strange happened. A girl was there with a small puppy on a leash and I bent down to pet it. It could see me. The dog started jumping up on me and the girl tugged at his leash, but he kept jumping. The dog jumped so high I had to catch him and ended up flipping him upside down as I was putting him on the ground.

You're Welcome

"How'd you do that?" she said out loud.

However, now there were two dogs. To make sure I flipped the dog again and there were three dogs. I believe she could only see the one she had on a leash but there were no leashes on the two new dogs and they ran off perhaps before she saw them. Maybe animals were different than other items I replicated.

I heard Sam say she was getting cold and was going back to look for her mom. We caught up with her in front of a furniture store where she was discussing buying something new for her house. That's what window shopping was all about, dreaming.

I walked ahead and looked in the window at the toy store. It was too early to be looking for next year but there in the middle of the window was my Magnetel pool table. I already had that! I saw Sam and the rest of the family heading back to the parking lot. We must be leaving. I ran to catch up but as I ran I noticed that I was above the ground. Not flying, somehow when I ran, the distance between my legs was much larger than normal. It was like running in space. I don't know how else to describe it.

I didn't notice it when I ran from the house with my backpack to the fireplace and then to the back gate where I found Sam's note, but I don't think I had entered the altered realm yet. I decided to test it. I slowed down and was walking normally and I ran a little bit and nothing happened. I tried to run a little faster, still nothing. Then I ran like I was when it happened and sure enough I was space running again. How cool was that. I'd have to share that with Sam. I thought I would keep the dog thing to myself because somehow, maybe, I could use that to surprise her. I caught up with them in no time at all and wasn't even tired. We were on our way back to her Aunt's. That was only day two.

Sam laughed when I told her about space running and said that I needed to test it out more. Like run so fast and see how far I could go. She thought I should run beside the car when we were driving home at least until we stopped for lunch. I didn't think that was a very good idea. "If I try it again, I'll see how tired I get." I wrote on the pad.

We wrote and talked all about the play and the ice cream and the park and stayed up most of the night. Tomorrow was going to be our second Christmas day, so we could sleep a little later. I got my pajamas on and both of us fell asleep. I had the most wonderful dream about fairies.

Chapter Ten

We slept late that next morning and no one bothered to wake us up. It was almost eleven by the time we went downstairs. Neither of us was very hungry. When we woke up Sam asked me if it was going to bother me that I didn't get any presents today when they were celebrating. I wrote that I had already had my Christmas and that she should enjoy herself. I told her that I thought I might leave the house for the day and see what adventure I could find. She said to go, and she would look for signs that I was back. We still had three more days and she said, "Be back in time to go home."

I took an apple from the fruit basket and left. Sam would tell me about her day later. I wasn't sure where I would end up, but I thought I might see if anyone was on the river ice fishing. Her Aunt's house had so much land that you could walk for blocks between neighbors. From the back door of the house there was a stone path that weaved in and about many trees down to the river. It had snowed during the night and everything was covered in new fluff. All the old dirty snow along the coast was gone and I wished I had a camera. I need to remember to test the theory of me showing up in a picture.

As I walked closer to the river I saw they had a fairly large boathouse and behind it was a dock. The boats were in the boathouse for the winter though. I also saw there was an ice shanty on the river. I had been in my dad's many times when he went ice fishing on Turtle Lake. They blocked the wind and his had a small buddy heater in it. Sometimes though when he opened the door the wind would blow out the pilot light and he would have to light it again. It made fishing in winter a fun sport and kept your nose from freezing. I didn't see anyone around, so I decided to make snow angels.

After a while I got tired of what I was doing and started walking on the river. It seemed as good a time as any to test my running theory. I started running until I got my speed up and headed out over the river. I was space running before long and the faster I ran in the space the farther I went. I was less than a foot above the ground but didn't need to touch it to move. I ran until I reached the other side of the river. I'm guessing it was about four or five miles across and took about seven minutes which wasn't bad. If I had known about it when I got stuck downtown I could have made it back to my house in about forty-five minutes. I didn't have a watch to time myself and decided I would add that to my backpack when I got back. I also wasn't tired which was a good thing.

When I got to the other side there were some people ice fishing and children ice skating. I went over to where they were fishing and watched them for a while and when they got ready to leave, I picked up a few of the fish and put them down again so they had a few more for supper. Not too many though because I knew there were laws about the number of fish you could catch. I also followed them. Some of the kids went with one man and woman so I jumped in their jeep with them. I had no inkling where I was going but if I got back to the river I would remember how to get back.

We didn't drive for too long before we came to the St. James Hotel. It was a very old four-story building. Rich in history it was an old-world Italianate structure. I read that on a brochure in the lobby. The hotel's first floor had three dining rooms, a kitchen, office and baggage storage while the lower level featured a parlor, billiard hall, barbershop, public baths and four bathrooms for men. The second floor featured a lady's parlor, bridal suite and two bathrooms. An elegant ballroom occupied the fourth floor.

Listening to conversations I found out the couple I went there with works for the Red Wing Shoe Factory and were there for the New Year's festivities that would take place at the end of the week. We would be back home for New Year's Day, but I did get to go with them for hot chocolate and see the fireworks they have every night.

S. M. Anker

The hotel was down river from where I needed to be, so I used my space running to leave. I'm guessing it took less than fifteen minutes and I was back. I had to crawl in Sam's sister's bedroom window which they left open to let in the fresh air. A few minutes in the bathroom and up to the bedroom I went. Sam was sleeping already. She didn't even feel me get into bed. Sleep came easy.

I slept most of the next day away, except to use the bathroom, and didn't get up until after supper. I don't know if it was the space running or fresh air that made me tired or if it was the entire experience. I managed to get downstairs as they were leaving for the St. James Hotel. I had to laugh.

When we got there I saw the couple that I was with the day before. They were also walking into the hotel restaurant. I never saw a more elegantly furnished place to eat. One side of the room had an antique mahogany bar with a corner brick fireplace that had fire dancing in the hearth. Deep velvet Chesterfield couches finished off the space. I had also read that in the brochure. There were many people sitting having drinks while they waited for a table for supper. Sam's Aunt had a reservation, so we were escorted to our table within minutes of our arrival.

The dining area was a very large space. In the middle area of the room sat another fireplace that was visible from both sides of the room. It too was lit. All the tables in the room were round and different sizes. If you had a large group, you could sit at a table that could fit up to sixteen people. Our group had nine, so we sat a table big enough for ten. Each round table had something called a 'Lazy Susan' in the middle with a cold-water pitcher, salt, pepper, and condiments for sandwiches, coffee, and extra napkins. I thought it would be great to have one of those for our kitchen table at home. I'd have to talk to my dad about that.

The table had a gold linen tablecloth with crystal glassware. One glass was for water and the other for wine. At least that is what I saw on the other tables. The silverware was very fancy. All silver with touches of gold around a pressed pattern of peacocks. Everyone had two knives, two spoons and three different types of forks. I was going to eat with the silverware I brought from my backpack, but I watched to see what the others did with the silverware. I would remember when I got older.

The ceiling had streamers and large four-foot round gold balls and was decorated for the New Year's celebration. Later after supper we went up to the ballroom where we had tickets for a pre-New Year's Eve party for younger children. I had stayed up talking half the night on many occasions when I had sleep overs but had never been up at midnight for New Years. Sam whispered that they had the clocks turned ahead so that we would celebrate midnight but that it would be around eight o'clock. They didn't want the children out that late. I had so much fun and got to dance and drink eggnog.

You're Welcome

Closer to our fake midnight they passed out princess tiaras for the girls to wear and top hats for the boys and streamers to throw and these things that you blew on and they unrolled and made noise. It was all quite exciting and then they set up a late-night dessert table. Sam was allowed one sweet, but I had three different kinds. One was a chocolate éclair, then I had some cheesecake with strawberries and whipped cream. I saved the best for last, bread pudding with something called Vanilla Cream Brule sauce on top of it. After everyone had their fill of sweets, we were led to an outside veranda to watch fireworks. It was an amazing evening that I never want to forget.

Later when we got back to the house we had so much to talk about. I told her that I didn't get tired when I was space running, but that I had slept most of the next day and didn't know if it was from the fresh air or the running and that I needed to explore that further. She made the observation that the Sas back home was sure missing out on some special memories. I sure hoped when this all ended, I was the one that kept them. When I told her, I had three desserts, she wondered if I was eating and my other self was also eating would I get fat. I told her I had thought that myself and that if she noticed I was gaining weight she should tell me.

After we had breakfasted the next morning, we went to visit the same relatives that had come for her second Christmas, only this time at their homes. We spent a little time at each house and had milk and cookies at the first house and supper at the second house and the relatives from the first house came with us. Everyone ended up at the last house for pie and ice cream. All the grownups played cards. Sam and I and some of her cousins watched television. It was about ten when we got into the car and headed back. Sam fell asleep first, then her Mom, and finally me.

We left for home the next morning after Aunt Marie fixed us the most fantastic

You're Welcome

going away breakfast. We had eggs over easy, waffles with maple syrup, sausages and bacon, chocolate milk, and fried potatoes. I was stuffed by the time we left and didn't know why anyone would have to stop for lunch on the way home. They did though. I passed and stayed in the car sleeping while they were eating. I don't know how any of them found room to put one more morsel into their stomachs.

I looked at Sam's watch when she came back to the car and it was after two. We would be home in about three and a half hours and I wasn't very anxious to get there. It would be nice if this could continue.

I had a short paper conversation with Sam when we got back to her house, grabbed my pillow and told her I would call her when I got home. Supper would be over already. I made a quick trip to get a fish sandwich and fries and left the money on the counter. When I got back to the house I wasn't sure where I would have to enter. The neighbor's fireplace wasn't glowing, so I walked into the house. I left my backpack lying on the ground on the other side of Sam's Aunt's house so the only thing I had to put away was my pillow and throw the cases down the clothes chute. I did take a quick glance to make sure my backpack was still under the stairs and that's when I noticed the clothes chute glowing and pulsating. I climbed in and dropped to the basement and reached my hand through the slot and opened it.

I guess I was back then. I walked upstairs, and Mom said, "I thought you were watching television." I said, "I was, but I wanted an orange soda and there wasn't any in the fridge." I got some ice out of the freezer, poured the soda, and walked into the living room. I wasn't there. I walked back into the kitchen and gave my Mom a big hug. She asked, "What was that for?" I said, "I have no idea."

I decided to grab my backpack anyway on the way up to put my pajamas on. I took everything out and repacked it adding a watch that I hadn't worn in a while. I grabbed another clean towel since I had decided one wasn't enough and two extra pillowcases then put the backpack back under the stairs.

I had to run back upstairs. I had, seen it then. There was a phone in the hallway on the wall. Beneath it was a chair with a table top and a turquoise colored padded back. It must have been put in during the week I was away. I had to act like I knew it was there but to be sure, I went down and asked Mom if it was okay if I used it. She said, "That is what it's up there for."

I smiled and ran back upstairs and dialed Sam. "Hey, purple socks here." She said, "Oh good you got back okay." I told her about the new phone and we talked for about an hour before Arthur told me to get off so he could use it. I was back in the real world and there was no getting away from the fact that other people lived here.

Chapter Eleven

New Year's Eve came and went without much celebration, but I had already had mine. We were still out of school for a few more days and spent most of it skating at the park. That was cool. When we went back to school it wasn't together. I went to a school that I was bused to and she went to the old school we had gone to together. When I was entering sixth grade the school asked parents to voluntarily send one of their children to a new school behind the tracks. We had nine kids, so my parents had to volunteer one of us. I got elected.

I can't say I was happy about it. I had to leave all my friends behind at the old school and get up earlier to catch the bus on the corner across the street from the Water Fall. I had met lots of new friends, but I was still disappointed that I couldn't talk to Sam everyday like before. I still had one more year after this one and then instead of going to high school, I would be going to a junior high. There were plans to build a new high school beginning next year sometime. I'd have to go to another school first before I got there. It couldn't happen fast enough.

When we finally did go back to school Sam was not as available as she had been. She was taking special classes that took up more of her time and because she was a little older than me, she and some of her other friends started hanging out without me.

Most of the month was spent practicing the music for our Spring Choral. We had eight new songs to learn by the beginning of April and sometimes the teacher would let me play for the class. I was starting to write piano music in my lessons and loved practicing at the school because the acoustics in the music room were wonderful.

On Saturdays I went to my piano lessons and it was about an hour ride each way to get there. Dad took me unless he was working and then I took the bus. Sometime before my last birthday, my father made a knitting spool and I used it on my way to and from my lessons. It was made from wood and was about five inches long and about two inches in diameter. There was a hole drilled through the length of it in the middle about a half inch in diameter. On the top of the spool there were four little metal posts. I have to drop a piece of yarn through the hole until there is a 'tail' coming out the bottom and then wrap yarn around the posts in a zigzag pattern and use a crochet needle to pull and loop the yarn over the posts. I keep looping and pulling on the tail and before long there is a yarn rope coming out the bottom. I was probably the only one at school with a handmade spool.

It was popular to take an empty spool of thread and make one by putting four small nails in the top. Mine was way better and so much more special because my dad had made it. He had originally made it for Amelia, but she wasn't using it any more so now it's mine. Nanny gave me yarn that was left over from some sweater, scarf, or afghan that she had made so my rope was many different colors and textures. Nanny taught me how to crochet when I was seven years old but since I got the spool, I haven't crocheted anything. I had no idea what I was going to do with the rope or how long I was going to make it. I'd say it was about fifteen feet so far.

I called Sam to see if she wanted to go downtown with me on the bus one Saturday later in the month after my lesson, but she had signed up to go on a mission retreat for our catechism class and wouldn't be home. She hadn't told me about it and her whole family was going to do it.

I needed to make my own arrangements and wondered if the couple next door that I made rosaries with did anything like that. I was leaving to go ask and Mom stopped me. "Where are you going?" I told her, and she said, "They moved yesterday while you were at school, there is another couple moving in tomorrow with two young daughters."

S. M. Anker

Now what was I going to do. I talked it over with Mom and she thought that maybe our neighbors on the other side of the house knew of something. They were very faithful church goers and I had spent lots of time playing with their daughter. I asked, and they said that if I wanted to go to church with them I could. The next day instead of going to my church I went to a church in the city. I went with the intent of finding a mission program to become a part of but instead, I found out that they were moving. Someone had purchased their home and they were going to build a new bank on the property. I was bummed about this startling news. Later next month some big company was going to move her house to a lot near the park where we skated. That would be interesting to watch. The new bank would be opened later in the year and I wondered what that would be like.

When I got home, Mom was in the basement washing clothes and ironing. When I told her about the neighbors she

You're Welcome

told me that she and my dad had already known. I was actually pretty mad at them for not saying anything but didn't let on. Instead I asked Mom if she needed any help with the ironing. "Go play until supper is ready, but thanks."

"You're welcome." After I said it, Arthur came down the stairs into the basement giggling, then left.

Immediately I began to feel sick. The feeling was always the same, nausea without being able to get sick physically. I was becoming accustomed to it but each time it still took me by surprise on how fast it happened. I looked around to see if anything was glowing. It was the door to the bathroom. First thing I did was run upstairs and grab my backpack. I made sure I put the watch on and headed back to the basement. I had taken the money out of the backpack because I wanted to see if money was different in the altered realm like the dogs in the park had been. I also remembered not to take my pillow. I would replicate that afterwards. That way I would have my pillow in both worlds. I could see Mom across the room still ironing clothes, so I slowly made it to the bathroom unnoticed.

Once inside it was clear that I had to crawl under the stairs to the creepy place. I crunched down and went all the way to the opening that took me into the area under the stairs that led to the basement. This area was glowing brighter and I could feel its pulse. As I turned the corner I shouldn't have been able to, but I could stand up and as I walked forward I was on the corner where I caught my bus for school.

As I looked across the main street I noticed a train stopped on the tracks behind the factory that was there. I decided I would walk over there, but first I went back to the house and picked up my pillow and squeezed it into the backpack and put the money in my pocket. As long as they were connected to me in some way, they could not be seen.

I walked back up to the corner and waited until traffic let up a little and walked across the street toward the train.

You're Welcome

Trains that left the factory always went to the Chicago yard to link up with trains going all over the country.

I decided if I could find an open freight car I would take a short trip to Chicago. I crossed the track at the front of the train and started walking up the side of it facing away from the main street toward the back until I found an open car. I threw my backpack up into it and hoisted myself up. I was physically in pretty good shape so getting into the car wasn't much of a task. It would probably take about three hours to get to Chicago but I didn't know when it would leave, so I settled in and got ready for the ride. After what seemed like hours, I glanced at my watch and it was ten after three. Hardly any time had elapsed. The whirr of the locomotive confirmed we were going to be moving soon. I could hear the hiss of pressure building up and as we pulled out, the steady clickity clack, clickity clack, across the tracks reminded me of the sound my roller skates made when I skated in front of the shoe store. It was very calming and rapidly lulled me to sleep.

I woke up when I heard the whoo, whoo of the engine whistle as we were making a turn in the bend and checked my watch and it was five. When I looked out the freight car door it was starting to get dark. I could still make out the silhouettes of the trees as we passed by and the sky had a crimson radiance to it. It looked like it was going to be a wonderful night. We were maybe another half hour from the train station where the Chicago North Shore Line would bed for the night before making the connections needed. I'd be able to get to downtown Chicago on a bus from the station so I stayed awake the rest of the trip so I would be able to jump off as soon as it stopped. Otherwise I might sleep the entire night away and be half way across the country when I woke up.

We pulled into the station around five minutes to six and as soon as it was safe, I jumped down. I saw four others getting off the train as well. Maybe I would share a car with someone on the way back. For

You're Welcome

now, my goal was to find the bus that would take me into the downtown area. I saw a few people standing at a bus stop and decided to space run over to where they were. When the next bus came it was indeed going in my direction. I grabbed some of the change I had in my zippered compartment and put it into the change box as I was getting in. I tried to time it so that when the person in front of me put their fare in the box, mine would slide down with it. The bus driver didn't notice, but the guy in front of me did.

There were plenty of empty seats on the bus so I sat around the middle; hoping most of the people would prefer the back. It took about twenty minutes to reach the downtown area. I picked a stop near what looked like a new building to get off and went inside to find a bathroom to use. According to a plaque I saw inside, it had only opened and it smelled new. When I came out of the bathroom I followed some men into the elevator and hit the highest numbered button there was. Everyone got off and I kept going until my floor.

S. M. Anker

When I stepped off the elevator there was a door off a small hallway. I tried the door expecting it to be locked, but it wasn't. I turned the knob and opened it. On the other side was a set of stairs leading up. Being inquisitive, I took the stairs until I reached another door. When I opened it I saw the night sky.

Now, I knew I probably was not supposed to be up there, but the doors were open so I stepped out onto the roof. I walked around the edge of the building which had a three foot high, brick edging around it. I had never been on the roof of any building, let alone one that was over fifty stories tall. The view was absolutely amazing and I could feel the wind blowing across the top of the building but was glad I couldn't feel the temperature. The evening lights from the city were simply glorious. Looking down toward the sidewalks below, I could see little people walking and the tiniest cars moving about. I had never been up in an airplane but figured that is how it would probably look.

You're Welcome

I actually got a little dizzy looking down so I decided to check out the roof some more. I started where I came out of the door, which I checked again to make sure was still unlocked. There was an empty bag on the ground so I shoved it in near the bottom between the door and the frame so that it wouldn't close all the way. Moving to my right, I saw a bunch of steel beams piled up that looked like they had been abandoned there after the building was finished. The wind had obviously blown the snow in that direction as the snow was woven between the beams from previous storms. The rest of the roof was relatively clear of snow.

I walked around the beams and saw one torn mattress and a bunch of garbage consisting of empty cans from soda, pork and beans, and soup. I also saw some utensils and dishes lying around. Next to the mattress was a box. I peeked inside and found a small bowl, a blanket and a ton of newspaper. I'm guessing that someone was actually sleeping up there. I wondered what that would be like. A little further ahead I noticed a similar area. No mattress, but there was a box with stuff inside. This little area was scattered with Sterno cans. It looked to me like this person was burning them to stay warm.

I thought about my bed back home and how I took it for granted. This is something I would try to remember when I got older so I could perhaps be more compassionate towards people who did have to live like this. Most of the rest of the roof was the same. Little spaces niched out for each person that stayed there at night. I wondered how many made this their home.

That's what I was thinking when I heard some noise. I watched what happened in the next half hour with such intent that I thought I was watching a scripted television show. Two men came through the door. They appeared to be arguing and were yelling at each other. The argument lasted the entire time and eventually turned into a fist fight. They

You're Welcome

moved all around the roof banging into things, tripping over stuff and then clear out of the blue one of the men stopped in the middle of it all and started laughing. "You sure you want to do this?" he asked the other guy.

"Are you kidding, we have to do this, besides, it will be so much fun and when will we ever get another chance?"

"Okay then let's go or we'll be late."

That's all I needed. I had to go with them now to see what was going on and to find out why they had been fighting. What could these two be up to? I followed them down the stairs. Good for me that they stopped to use the bathrooms on the first floor. I looked at my watch and it was twenty before eight.

The men were definitely on a mission to get somewhere quickly and as much as they appeared to be enemies a few seconds ago, I couldn't tell it now. We walked across several streets and ended up in front of the Victoria Theatre. One of them opened their wallet and took out a couple of tickets. They were going in. I grabbed some of my allowance and tossed it up into the box office and I ran after them. They got to their seats and there were a couple empty ones close by so I sat down. There was a band already playing on the stage so I listened to them. I hadn't heard them before but thought they were pretty good. I kept watching to see if anyone was headed to the seat I chose but no one came. After about thirty minutes the band on the stage left and a new band came out. I didn't recognize any of them either.

The way the show was set up made it very cozy and intimate and as each announcement was made the crowd got more excited and the entire auditorium was standing up clapping now with anticipation. Then the show began. I thought to myself, I know that song. I could feel the energy in the audience.

I started to glance around, to my left and then my right and it was certain that these people were craving what was coming. There was a gargantuan scream

You're Welcome

deep inside me waiting to explode and I didn't even know why.

They made it all very mysterious when he actually came on stage and then it hit me. Oh my goodness. My heart was jumping out of my chest with the same excitement and I let go of that scream along with everyone in the place. I was without a doubt at an Elvis concert! He had been touring Paris in January and only now had returned to the states. How could he be there?

He had recently wrapped the movie, "Viva Las Vegas" and I was waiting for it to come out in May. I had already seen "GI Blues" and "Blue Hawaii." I wasn't a huge fan but I did like him some, and in person he was so much cuter. How could I deny how excited I was with a room full of screaming people?

All this went through my mind in about ten seconds and I settled in for the night of my life. It was going to be a keen concert. He was a great entertainer and I was still surprised that he was there. His career was mostly focused on his movies and the tickets for this concert must have been at least seven dollars. I had about four dollars left and one thing was for certain, when I went out during the break I would give them the rest of the money in my backpack. Well, almost all of it. I might need some later. Elvis was all over the stage. The backup singers and dancers may have been there to make the show better, but I wouldn't have cared if he was on the stage totally alone.

I glanced over to see how the two men I had followed there were enjoying the concert. From what I could tell they were having the time of their lives as well. The rest of the night was outta sight. He never stopped singing except to take a drink or towel off or settle in for a new song. When he was obviously tired from a song, he would find a place to sit and sing a few ballads. When it was over I checked my watch, like many did. He had been on that stage for over three hours.

Afterwards I followed the men to see where they were headed. They walked a bit retracing some of our original steps but then made a turn in a different direction. We ended up in front of a restaurant called Beat the Clock. We went in and they were seated. I ducked into the bathroom to wash up and then joined them. I came back as the waitress was repeating their order. Please, please, have ordered onion rings I thought to myself.

"That'll be two cheeseburgers with grilled onions, mayo, pickles, and tomato; one chocolate malt, one cherry cola; a large order of onion rings and a regular order of fries."

"Will that do it for you?"

"Yes," they said "That's it for now, maybe we will have dessert later."

"Be up in a jiffy." She said as she made her way back to the kitchen.

The guys started talking as they waited. It turns out that if you eat in this restaurant and they don't bring you your food within five minutes, the food is on the house. Now, the name of the place made sense to me. They were watching the time while they were talking and as they saw her coming out with the food the five minute deadline had already passed. One of them told her "We beat the clock, it has been more than five minutes." She went back into the kitchen for a minute and came back out with the drinks and a check that had been totaled out with a zero balance.

Then we ate. I knew if I picked up the food from their plates they wouldn't miss any of it so I grabbed a burger, chocolate malt, and of course the onion rings. I hadn't thought about eating all night, but was starving. At that moment I again thought, 'I better not gain weight from all this extra food.'

I ate about half of the onion rings and when they were done eating they ordered hot fudge sundaes and I enjoyed that. Glad I brought my spoon with me. During dessert, I learned that they were business men and that they had been playing cards earlier in one of the suites on the twenty-second floor and had won the concert tickets in the game. They had gotten into a fight with the guy who lost

You're Welcome

the tickets, so they tried to leave. They decided to go up in the elevator instead of down because that's the way the guy they were fighting with would go to catch them. What I saw when they came up wasn't a real fight, it was like they were recreating the fight from downstairs. So it happens that they ended up on the roof for kicks. Their kicks ended up being my treasure.

When we were finished, the waitress handed them a bill for the desserts and thanked them for their free meal. I know I didn't understand what she was saying, but they talked about it on the way out. I guess when you eat any free food the waitress that messed up the order pays for it out of their wages.

I didn't feel that was fair and I never had a chance to give most of my money back to the box office because there never was an intermission, so I reached into my pocket and grabbed most of it and ran back inside and left it on the table for a tip hoping that would help her out. She saw the money and I saw her mouth to them as they left, "Thank you."

When I got back outside they were ahead of me going into a nearby hotel and I saw them get a key from the front desk. I was tired, so I headed back to the building where I started. It was still opened so I used the bathroom and headed to the elevator. When I got to the top of the stairs the paper bag I placed in between the door and the frame wasn't there. I tried the door and to my surprise, it was still unlocked. I opened the door and what I saw shocked me. There were about fifteen people up there. Sterno cans were aflame, someone had a small transistor radio playing; one woman was stirring something in a pot. All of them must live on the roof. It was funny because as I was thinking that, The Drifters came on the radio singing "Up on the Roof," a song they had released about a year or so earlier. I sang along for a while and so did most of the people up there listening. It was a great song and as I managed to make myself a place to sleep, I wondered

You're Welcome

what stories these nomads could tell. I listened to them talking and watched them for a long time, but without any warning, I nodded off.

When I awoke, everyone was already gone. The Sterno cans had been put out, but I managed to eat from the few morsels of sausage and potatoes that they left in a pan until I was full. It also looked like they had straightened up. I guess this was their home and they at least tried to treat it like it was. And now, I found myself wanting to get to mine.

I was going to leave my pillow behind somewhere anyway, so I picked it up and set it down about twenty times so there would be pillows for everyone when they came back later that night. I explored the museums and stores killing time and I headed back to catch the bus around supper time. I grabbed a sandwich from a nearby deli first. Once I was in the train yard I spotted the train going back towards my house and waited to see if anyone else was getting on. I didn't see anyone, so I jumped up into a car. It took about an hour and I was on my way before six o'clock. The whole trip was uneventful and when I got back, I went to the basement first, but didn't see that was where I needed to go back to the real world. I looked all over and fell asleep on the glider on the patio. It was after ten when I woke up to the sound of some of Arthur's friends cutting through the yard. The back door was still unlocked so I checked the bathroom again and this time it was glowing and pulsating. I started crawling into the creepy place again and as I crawled, I was actually coming out of the kitchen cabinet dresser in my bedroom. Everyone was sleeping.

You're Welcome

Chapter Twelve

At the beginning of February, Sam called, and we talked. I asked her how her mission trip to Montana went and she told me all about it. Other than the trip she said school was a challenge but wanted to know what I had been up to. I told her all about Chicago. Before we hung up she told me her school was having a dance for Valentine's Day and asked if I want her to get me a ticket. I told her that would be fun and for sure to get one for me. We planned to get ready for the dance at her house.

The day before the dance it snowed hard all day and dumped about thirteen inches of the white wet stuff. The school board was going to cancel it altogether, but the moms belonging to the Parent Teacher Association had already decorated the gymnasium with bales of hay and corn stalks and hung red and white streamers. They were also the ones responsible for preparing the punch and treats that were being served and I was pretty sure they didn't want any of the food to go to waste. They made calls to the School Board that it would be a shame to cancel. The plows had done a good job clearing the sidewalks and the roads were clear, so the Board listened to them. Besides most of them had children that were looking forward to it.

Everyone brought their forty-five rpm records and a few of the fathers made sure the music never stopped. Someone had even brought a few Beatles songs. In the last week it seemed like that was all the radio would play. They were on the Ed Sullivan show the week before. Since the show the news kept showing this picture of a girl in the audience, in black glasses, that looked like me and everyone kept asking me what it had been like to see them in person. I got tired of explaining that it wasn't me. This dance hadn't been any different.

Around seven thirty I asked Sam if she planned on going anywhere at eight when the dance was finished, and she said her dad was taking a few of them up to the

You're Welcome

Dairy Dutch. Burgers cost seventy-five cents which included an onion haystack, and a soda. It was on the other side of town though and I didn't want to go that far. I was still saving my allowance for future adventures, so I stayed and helped the cleanup committee pick up cups and napkins from the tables before I headed home. As I was leaving one of the parents yelled out to me, "Thanks for helping." I said, "You're welcome." It came out of my mouth so fast.

Here we go again. I had gotten only as far as the mailbox on the corner across the street from the school and it started glowing. I wondered what would happen if I ignored it. I was tired from all the dancing, so I started walking home. I went up to my bedroom and got ready for bed. What would happen if I didn't go this time?

Amelia was still awake reading one of her glamour magazines. I asked her if I could talk to her and she said "Sure."

"I was wondering about the time you covered for me when I crawled in the house through the milk chute." "Why did you tell me no one was watching?"

"What are you talking about?" she asked.

"I was wondering if you were looking out for me and if you knew what was going on."

"I have no idea what you are talking about, go to bed." I thought, what if she had been on her own adventure and she had gotten back from hers but hadn't returned yet. But how could she see me in my adventure? Was I still in the altered realm when she saw me? All this thinking was making my head hurt. I said, "That's okay, never mind, thanks."

Amelia said, "You're welcome." and I know I heard her giggle.

"What's up with the laughing all the time?" She looked at me and said that she didn't know, but she felt like laughing all of a sudden. I said, "You're welcome," and she giggled. I said it over and over and over about ten times and she was giggling so hard she almost fell off her

You're Welcome

bed. I'd have to talk to Sam about it tomorrow. I was still feeling sick, but I had decided that I wasn't going anywhere so I went to bed.

It seemed like no sooner did I lie down, the bed started pulsating. I ignored it for a while, but it was obvious that it was not going to let me go to sleep. I can honestly say that I was freakin' out a little because the bed felt mad. They were my adventures, it was my wish, and tonight I didn't want to go anywhere. I wanted to go to sleep. My mind wouldn't turn off. If I eventually had to go was I going to have the same adventure I would have if I had gone right away? Would there be a new place to enter the altered realm. Just because the bed was pulsating didn't mean I was leaving, it had something to do with the glowing place as well. I wondered if it would all end before I figured out how it all worked.

The bed did not stop. I got up and went to get the backpack. I had laundered the clothes after my trip to Chicago and had it ready. I knew I was going to have to come back each time for my pillow and money. Last trip I had gotten my money after I entered the altered realm and people could see the money as soon as I let go of it so I could pay for things. I had gotten fifty cents from Nanny for Valentine's Day which would help. When I got back the bed wasn't pulsating any longer. Now what? As soon as I made myself comfortable it started up again and I got back up.

"Oh, for the life of me, what is going on?" My sister yelled at me.

"Nothing, I'm having trouble getting to sleep." Amelia told me to go downstairs and make some hot chocolate. "It will help you relax and be quiet when you come back, I'm going to bed and don't wake your sisters." I went downstairs.

My parents had gone to bed at ten, so I was very quiet. The back door started pulsating. "Okay, Okay," I mumbled under my breath. I went upstairs and

You're Welcome

grabbed my stuff. Amelia had already fallen asleep. I left my pillow and money on the patio glider for later.

I realized I was freezing and in my pajamas. The sidewalk was pulsating, and I followed it. I should have run back for my coat but knew if I did leave I wouldn't need it. I hoped no one saw me and that it would happen before I caught my death of pneumonia.

I walked quickly along the sidewalk, each stone square I was on would stop pulsating and the square stone in front of it would start. It was taking me right towards Sam's school, back to the mailbox.

Once I was standing in front of it, the entire box started pulsating, then the door where you put the letters into the box was glowing. I put my hand on it and opened it up.

I felt a tug and the next second, I was inside a black dark space. As I slowly walked forward it was becoming light again. There was a door. I opened it and I was on the street outside the school right where I was two hours earlier after cleaning up after the dance and I wasn't cold any longer. A few stragglers were coming out after me saying goodnight to each other. Had I gone back in time then, I wondered. If I had then Sam would still be up at the restaurant. I thought I would space run up there. I dug down into my backpack for the watch I had packed and put it on. It was eight forty-five. I had gone back in time. I'd have to share that with Sam first chance I got.

I ran in space back to the house to get my pillow and money off the glider then I took off and was standing in the parking lot at the restaurant in no time. Two minutes and ten seconds had gone by according to the watch. *'Too bad I couldn't go out for the track team next year'.*

I peeked in the window and spotted Sam and a bunch of her friends in the third section of booths. I walked in and had to get her attention. Or did I? She knew I hadn't intended on going there so she wouldn't expect me to be there.

You're Welcome

I hung out for a while with them and saw my sister Amelia enter. She was with several of her girlfriends and I sat down in the empty seat at their table. I didn't understand a single word they were saying though. They were talking some made up language that they created so they could talk in public around other people and no one would understand what they were saying. I had heard it before at the house. If she was on the phone and I was walking by she would transfer to this quirky language. It wasn't any fun not knowing what they were discussing. I got bored stiff and went outside.

I watched some of the older bus boys shoveling snow in the back of the restaurant. When it snowed yesterday the plows had blocked in the dumpsters, so they were trying to clear a path. Then I figured since I hadn't wanted to have an adventure tonight, I'd make it a short one. As I was headed out the door, I noticed the fish tank. It had been there a long time. When I was much younger it was in the Falls Tavern that sat on the corner where the Water Fall is now. The cousins that bought the land didn't think the tank was the right thing for a burger joint. The Dairy Dutch bought the tank from the owners before it was torn down. It was a good time to test my animal theory. I counted how many fish were in the tank. Fourteen exactly, so I grabbed one up in my hand and then threw it back in, fifteen exactly. I did that a few more times until there were seventeen fish in the tank. I found a napkin and wrote, "How many fish are in the tank?" and slipped it into Sam's pocket. When she was finished eating she put her hand in the pocket to get her mittens and found the note. After reading it she went and counted the fish and softly said fourteen. It had worked. Replicated animals were not seen in the real world like other objects. The girl in the park had not seen the two dogs that ran away.

Since I wasn't cold, and it was a nice night out, I decided to walk home. On the way I saw a young woman standing next

You're Welcome

to her car crying. I stood there for a while and watched. Another girl came up to her and asked if she was alright. She told her that she had her key in her hand one minute and then it was gone. Somewhere in the snow around her it was buried. They both reached around in the snow for a while, but their hands were getting too cold to continue. Wow, I thought I could do that for a long time because the snow wouldn't bother me. If I could find her keys I could make her night better. However, if I found her keys I would also probably have an extra set. Maybe I could take them with me and dispose of them somehow. I didn't want an extra set of keys floating around for someone else to find and use. She could get her car stolen and if her house key was on the same ring it could be awful. Let's first see if I could find them. I moved over to where they were standing trying to get their hands warmed up.

I shoved my hand in the snow and maneuvered through it. I tried to do it systematically. I went as far down to the

S. M. Anker

ground as I could. Some of the snow under the new snow was crusty and hard and I thought a set of keys would not have penetrated through it. That left about eleven or twelve inches I had to check. I tried to do it so they would not see the snow moving as I went through it. The truth is, I didn't know if they would see the snow moving. I looked through areas about twelve inches square and then moved on. I vaguely remembered her coming out of one of the doors as I had been crossing the street before I saw her crying. I worked toward that site. About seven feet later, I felt something touch my hand. Before I pulled it up out of the snow I tried to feel to make sure it was some keys. It felt like it was. As I started to pull it forward in my right hand, I also tried picking up the keys in my left. I was either going to have two sets of keys with one left in the snow or because one set of keys was connected to me as I picked up the other one, I would have both without another replication. When I was finished I had two sets of keys and yeah, another

You're Welcome

was still in the snow. Well that didn't work, but at least I could make sure she got one set back.

I went to her car and tried the lock. They were hers. I put one set of keys in my pocket and moved closer to her. I dropped the keys as close to her foot as I could and waited. It worked, she bent down to wipe away some snow and spotted the keys. She picked them up and showed the other girl and I heard her ask "Do you need a ride anywhere?" "Yeah," she said, "I was going to wait for the bus, but if you are offering I'll take it." I still had an extra set of keys to get rid of and had no clue what would happen to the set still in the snow.

One thing I did know, it felt good that I was able to help and for the girl who lost the keys, it felt good that someone else stopped to help her, enough to give her a ride. It was a good night all around, and helped me better understand when Mom said, *'one good turn deserves another.'* I was tired so I space ran back to the mailbox. It wasn't pulsating. The door to the school was and had a faint glow. I opened the door and as I walked in I found myself walking straight out of the closet across from my brother's room.

I had finished putting my backpack under the stairs when I heard Mom in the bathroom and waited on the stairs for her to come out. I scared the wits out of her, but she didn't say so. "What are you doing back up?"

"I was going to make myself some hot chocolate." She said, "Go ahead, but be quiet so your father doesn't wake up."

We always had two kinds of chocolate in the house. One can of Ovaltine and one jar of Kraft Malted Milk mix. I warmed some milk in a small kettle on the stove and added the malted milk mix. It was my favorite of the two choices. After I poured it into a cup, I put some marshmallows on top and went straight to bed when I was finished. I was relaxed now and so very tired. I hadn't had much of an adventure, only a good experience

You're Welcome

and I did learn something about the altered realm.

After school was over the next day I went by the Dairy Dutch and counted the fish. There were fourteen. I called Sam and told her what had happened and asked her if she knew it was me at the Dairy Dutch last night.

"Yeah, when I got the note I knew. So how long were you there? Were you spying on me?"

I told her "No, I didn't plan on going anywhere, but it wouldn't let me go to sleep." I explained about the sidewalk and mailbox and everything. I told her I didn't want to intrude on her while she was with all her other friends. She said she had a great time and told me all about it. Most of the conversation was about the dance. She told me when she got home her Mom gave her a message that Sas had called and wanted to know how it went, so she called me and has now told the story to both of us. She seemed a little annoyed though, so I asked, "Are you still okay with all this weirdness going on?"

She said it was getting a little confusing so maybe I wouldn't see her as often. With school we didn't see each other that often anyway, now she was saying it would be less than that. I didn't plan on calling her for a while. Between going to school, swimming class, piano lessons, babysitting, and catechism classes I stayed busy. When I wanted to go skating and stuff I went with my other friends from school. I didn't tell anyone else about my adventures because frankly I didn't think anyone would believe me. It was hard for me to believe.

You're Welcome

Chapter Thirteen

Winter continued to dump snow all over the place and it had gotten too cold to go out anywhere. Easter was also going to be early this year and the department store at the shopping center had an Easter Egg Contest going on. It had started in February immediately after the Valentines cards were packed away and would end March fourteenth. You had to decorate a hardboiled egg or two and then the judges would decide who came in first, second and third place. First place was a fifty-dollar savings bond and a large Easter basket. I didn't like art unless it was making something out of yarn and involved needles, but I liked competition and decided to give it a try.

My older sister's egg turned out cool. At school, she had won the sought-after title of Miss Teen Betty Crocker Homemaker for what she made through the high school Home Economics Department. How could she not win?

S. M. Anker

I did two eggs. I used toilet paper rolls and cotton and some yarn and other things Mom had in her sewing basket and made them into a bride and groom. I barely made the deadline but didn't have any expectation of winning. When we got the call that I did, I was surprised.

They made a big fuss over it and all the winners; first, second and third place, got to have their picture taken with their eggs in the store front window which was decorated for Easter. The pictures even made it into the local newspaper. It was a big deal for me, but I still thought that Amelia should have won. Mom said she would hold on to the savings bond I received until it matured, whatever that meant. I'd have to ask Dad about it.

I took the basket upstairs and opened it with Amelia. Inside there were two large chocolate rabbits. The wrapper said that they were solid milk chocolate. Most of the ones we got were hollow inside. These would last forever. I gave one of them to her. There were a ton of jelly beans and I

You're Welcome

divided those up for all the younger kids, all except the black ones. I kept those because I love black jelly beans almost as much as oatmeal and bread pudding.

There was a set of colored pencils and a book of color by number pictures. I told Amelia that she could pick out the ones she wanted and split the others between Helene and the twins. I gave the stuffed rabbit to Ellen. There were three packages of yellow and pink Marshmallow Peeps so I gave one to Richard, Arthur, and James. I didn't like them. On the other hand, there were also malted milk eggs. Oh my, how I loved the way they melted in your mouth. I gave Helene a few because I knew she liked them but kept the rest for myself. I also kept the diary and package of white tights. The bottom of the basket was loaded with jaw breakers, Charms, Abba Dabba taffy, Boston Baked Beans, and Necco wafers. I put all that in a bowl and took it downstairs to share with everyone. It had been a good day and when I looked out the bathroom window later, it was snowing again.

S. M. Anker

It was still two weeks until Easter and I had finally managed to find a short trip to complete for my confirmation. The nurse at the school had been speaking with my mom when she took my younger brother in for one of his shots. They knew each other well, with all the kids in the family, and the nurse had asked how I was getting along at the school behind the tracks. One thing led to another and before I knew it I was going to be going with her and her family and a bunch of people from her church to a small town's camp in Missouri that had flooded from a big storm. The trip would be next week Thursday and we would leave Wednesday after school. Spring vacation would begin so I wouldn't miss any school. I would however miss Easter at home. I didn't know how I felt about that.

The community center and other structures needed to be rebuilt and they needed as many hands as they could get. It was one of those trips were youth and adults were welcomed. I was looking forward to it. I wondered what the town

You're Welcome

would look like, how much damage there was and that night prayed for anyone that was injured and was affected by the damage. I was going to work as hard as I could to do my part.

The week went by fast as I prepared for the mission trip. We were told to wear jeans and to pack an extra pair if we had them. I also had to take something nice for church. I packed a green plaid jumper that Mom made me and a white turtleneck to go underneath it. I put the tights that I got in my Easter basket from winning the contest in as well. They didn't know for sure what the weather would be like so in addition to my pajamas, I packed a sweater, hat, scarf, my boots, mittens, tennis shoes, and my toothbrush. It dawned on me that I didn't have one or toothpaste in my backpack. I went downstairs right then and got them and put them in the backpack. Mom always had extra stuff like that in the linen closet. The church was going to provide us with t-shirts all four days we were there, so I only had to worry about the one I would wear while traveling and my coat.

As usual, I would take my pillow with me. They gave us the option if we wanted to. I put four cases on for the time we would be away. Mom wouldn't miss them because she was used to me taking extra cases. Nanny once told me I was peculiar when it came to my pillow and that someday I would be this little old lady with hundreds of unique pillowcases. Somehow, she understood. I mean who else gets pillowcases for their birthday.

Nanny had a small suitcase made from what I thought looked like ivory that she was going to let me use. It had a lock on it too. If the pillow and backpack wouldn't both fit, I'd carry the pillow. It didn't take long to finish putting everything in order and now I needed to wait until Wednesday.

School went fast Monday, Tuesday, and Wednesday and I was glad except for chorus practice. We would be giving our concert the week after the trip. I had been

You're Welcome

picked to sing alto in the Triple Trio and the teacher was making us work hard on our harmonies. The high school choir director told her that some representatives would be coming to our Spring Choral and if we were good enough we might be selected to go with the High School Choir to the State competition. We all wanted to go.

When I finally got home from school Wednesday, I changed my clothes into the ones that I picked out for the trip. I carried my pillow and suitcase downstairs and quickly grabbed the backpack from under the stairs and opened the suitcase to make sure it fit. It did. I put the stuff in the living room because Mom said when her friend came by for me I should be ready and could go out the front door. We never used the front door.

S. M. Anker

Chapter Fourteen

She was exactly on time. Mom gave me a kiss goodbye and handed me a small bag with some goodies inside. Daddy hadn't gotten home from work yet, but he had given Mom three dollars to give to me for the trip. I would put that in my zippered compartment.

This was going to be exciting. Mom's nurse friend drove up to the house in a Studebaker church bus. It was the color of a green apple with a large front window and looked like it would seat about thirty people. The front door opened and when I climbed up it was almost full, so I must have been the last person to be picked up. All the luggage and other stuff was piled into the last five rows of seats and someone took my suitcase, but I kept my pillow and snack bag with me and found an empty seat next to someone. She was sitting in the aisle seat and didn't want the window, so she got up to let me in. That was fine with me because I loved looking out the window.

You're Welcome

It would take under nine hours to get there and they wanted to get there by midnight. Everyone could get some sleep before going to work on Thursday morning. They had seven people who could drive so every hour or so someone else took the wheel. I had my snacks gone in the first two hours and by five o'clock I was hungry. The driver pulled the bus off the interstate and drove to a nearby park as I was thinking that. We all got out as it started to get dark. Several of the men were carrying boxes and a blue cooler.

Turns out the church women packed sandwiches for everyone and there were cans of soda in the cooler. Several boxes of chips were opened, and everyone helped themselves to a handful as they wanted them. It took all of about fifteen minutes for everyone to eat and another ten to use the bathrooms before we were back in the bus and on our way. Now that it was dark it didn't matter if I had a window seat, but everyone went back to the same seat they had. I propped up my pillow against the window and soon fell asleep.

It was another couple of hours later when I woke again and looked at my watch. It was almost nine thirty and we still had a few hours to go. I didn't feel sleepy now though. I wish I had brought my radio with me. Mom said I couldn't take anything personal along because I was there to do a job, not play. She clearly wasn't a traveler and didn't realize how boring it could get. The girl next to me had also been sleeping but was now wide awake as well. We played 'I spy' for a while until sleep took us both again.

A little after midnight we pulled into the camping area that we would be calling home for the next four days. We were guided by the adults into dormitory like rooms. Each room had a set of twelve bunks. There was one for the boys and one for the girls. The adults helped us with our luggage and we were told to get into our pajamas, use the bathroom and lights would be out in half an hour. They

You're Welcome

didn't give us one extra second. I fluffed my pillow and pulled up the blankets. The dorm hadn't been heated until we got there and turned it on and it would take some time until it warmed up. It would be nice and toasty by morning, which by the way didn't take long when you were sleeping so soundly.

When I go to school, there is usually a bunch of noise upstairs from my brothers and sisters and it acts like an alarm clock. I was not prepared to be woken that morning by a very obnoxious and loud cow bell. I knew the sound as soon as it started. Mom used a cowbell to call us into the house for lunch, supper or if she wanted us home. All the neighbors could hear it and if one mom or some other kid heard it they would look around for us and tell us to go home. I thought Mom was a mastermind when she started doing this. No one on the block except her did it so it worked. Now I was getting up to the same sound and I had to laugh to myself. Home, or the thought of it, seemed to follow me.

S. M. Anker

At the foot of every bunk it looked like the t-shirt fairy made a trip into the dorm while we were all sleeping. The whole place was bustling with people getting dressed, finishing up in the bathroom, and talking about what the day would bring. We were supposed to meet the boys at the mess hall when we were finished. It was a short fifteen-minute walk across camp. It was seven in the morning and the sun was out and the sky was crystal clear. No rain was in the forecast for the entire weekend. I was hungry.

I was surprised to see the ground was still a bit wet in areas from the flooding. Our dorm and the mess hall were built up on wood pallets and the floors were very dry. Most of the buildings that flooded too badly had been torn down and we were there to start putting the camp back together. When I walked into the dining room I hadn't expected so many people. We were asked to sit in a specific area and told that is where we would sit for the next four days.

You're Welcome

A man was standing at one end of the hall with a gavel and he pounded it hard on a nearby podium. Everyone got quiet. "Ladies and gentlemen, boys and girls, we want to welcome you to what we are now calling, Helping Hands Camp. We have over three hundred volunteers here for the weekend from seven different states. It is with much gratitude that I say you are a special group and we look forward to getting to know all of you much better while you are here. When we are finished with breakfast we will convene at the site of the community center which is on the map we placed at each table setting. Be prepared to work until the cowbell rings when we will meet back here for lunch. When you leave the mess hall there will be canteens of water for you to grab on your way out. Make sure you take one. Now, will Father Joseph please come up to lead us in prayer?"

Father Joseph was an older gentleman from the order of the Redemptorists in Northern Ireland. His prayer for us was short and to the point as he blessed the food and the work we were going to do.

Breakfast was simple and served buffet style. There were four large steel serving bins lined up on one side of the room. People could make their way down both sides of the table so twice as many people could be served at once. In the serving bins were scrambled eggs, bacon, sausages, and biscuits. Each table had salt and pepper, butter and jam on it. Once everyone had gone through the line at least once it was announced that if you wanted seconds you could. I was filled to the gills from my first plate of food. I spent the rest of the time talking to other kids and getting to know more about the camp.

Around eight o'clock we headed out the door for a morning of hard work. I grabbed a canteen on the way out and followed everyone else. They seemed to know where they were going so I didn't even look at my map. We walked for about twenty minutes toward the lake area and what we saw was almost too

You're Welcome

awful for words. The community center that once stood there wasn't. Part of the foundation was there and people from Otto's Concrete were already pouring cement. Our job would be to build the framework today for the entire building. Each adult took a handful of us kids to work with. I went with the guy who welcomed us at breakfast.

Then I was given a job to do. The person before me was going to drill a hole in a piece of wood and I was supposed to pick it up and put it together with a second piece that was longer and screw them together with a power screwdriver. They asked me if I thought I could do that, and I said, "If you show me one time I will." I have never been much of a book learning person. I always have better luck by doing it, or seeing someone else doing it, first. I had helped my father that way. He showed me, and I did it. I was a good follower. After the first one, he came and checked it out. "Good job, Sas, keep it up." I did.

S. M. Anker

The entire morning, I picked up a piece of two-foot wood, placed it together with a four-foot piece of wood, screwed them together and passed it on. Repeatedly I did this and could not imagine how it was all going to go together. I didn't need to worry about that though. If everyone did their little part, it would all work out. I was getting hungry as the cowbell rang. Lunch was served the same way as breakfast. We had hotdogs, French fries, a piece of fruit and some chocolate pudding. We were reminded to fill our canteens before we left for the afternoon. My arms were a little sore from the repetitive motions, but my upper body strength was better than most twelve-year-olds because of the swimming.

The afternoon went by fast. I started to see those piles of wood transforming into framework before my eyes. The cowbell rang around four-thirty as a half hour warning. It was almost time for supper. They didn't say if we would be working when we were through. I did know I was beat. I had to say a prayer that I would be

You're Welcome

able to make it. The food was good. We had roasted chicken, carrots, mashed potatoes and gravy, and dinner rolls. Everyone ate like there was no tomorrow. It's funny how a good day's work can build your appetite.

When we were done there was an announcement made to everyone. "Somehow Otto's Concrete has gotten their hands on some of the new flood lighting used on outdoor stages and has hooked them up for us so that we can work for two more hours. If we do, we will be able to move ahead first thing tomorrow with raising the frame. Is everyone in?" A swelling "Yes!" blurted out of the crowd and we all headed back towards the lake. It didn't even look dark out with those lights on, but when eight o'clock came around I was ready for bed, along with everyone else. We still had to walk back to the dormitory, change, and cleanup. I prayed my regular prayers that night, but added the one from earlier, "Please let my arms not be too sore in the morning." I don't remember even getting into bed.

The next day was another beautiful day. A bit warmer than the day before from what I felt on the way to the mess hall. I was happy to see we were having oatmeal, sausages, pancakes and fruit for breakfast. I did go back for seconds on the oatmeal and remembered to fill my canteen before I headed out.

I got a new job. This time I had to nail window frames together. After watching someone a couple of times, I was off and running. I was doing all the window frames for the entire center. Well, me and the guy I was working with. He didn't say how many that would be, but it was going to be quite a few based on the amount of wood that was on our pile. They checked a few of the first ones I did and then someone said, "No need to watch her, she's good." I said "Thanks."

I'd be lying if I said my arms were not sore despite the fact that I had rested the muscles all night. I continued all day, stopping for lunch around one when the

You're Welcome

cowbell rang. I couldn't believe how very hungry I was again. Lunch consisted of potato soup, corn muffins, salad fixings and fruit. When we got back to the site after lunch we were not looking at distinct piles of wood all over the ground. There was now an actual building. The guys had stayed behind when we went to lunch and raised the walls. Now as we were arriving they were headed for lunch. We finished the last window frame about the same time I heard the cowbell warning ring. Supper could not have come fast enough for any of us.

Tonight, we had pizza. There was regular cheese pizza, cheese pizza with mushrooms, cheese pizza with sausage, peppers, onions, and mushrooms, and the last kind had everything I could image on it. Since I was a cheese and mushroom girl, I headed for that line. I ate four slices which is more than I usually eat. Where was all this food going? My Dad would have said it was going in my bottomless pit. I had to laugh. I was even too tired to miss them.

S. M. Anker

We didn't have to go back to work after supper. Instead the camp had planned for us to have a bonfire sing-along. We even had an opportunity to make something called s'mores. We never had them at home, but Sam's mother made them once in a while, but she used marshmallow fluff instead of regular marshmallows and they were so messy. We stayed out until around eight and then hit the bunks. I had never worked so hard in my life. The night consumed me.

The cowbell was ringing and my watch said five o'clock in the morning. Are they joking, I thought. No, they weren't. We were given half an hour to get ready in the good clothes we brought, and we had to meet on the other side of the community center structure. We got down there about six as the sun was coming up. We were having an early Easter Christian Service in the most beautiful outdoor setting. I had forgotten it was Easter weekend. Chairs had already been set up in a semi-circle facing the water to the East so you could get the full experience of the sun rising. I

You're Welcome

loved the concept of having a service outdoors. I thought when I got home I would talk to my catechism teacher about doing one for the youth group.

After the service we got to stay where we were for breakfast instead of walking back to the mess hall. It was brought to us in one of the buses. We had burrito omelets. The tortillas were filled with a mixture of eggs, bacon, cheese and some had onions and others did not. I ate two of the burritos without onions, a banana, and a container of milk. We got a little extra time to eat and talk because we didn't have the long walk down from the mess hall. All the window frames I had made were now in place in the building as well as the doors. All the electrical and plumbing stuff had been finished yesterday as well as the framing for the roof. Today's project was getting the drywall up and the outside insulation and siding done. They were hoping to have it all done by the lunch bell.

My job today was steadying the drywall while someone else nailed it into the framing. It was remarkable how fast it all was happening and by the time the cowbell rang we were done. During lunch, which was burgers with or without cheese, onion rings, soda, and fruit, we found out that during all of our meals the city planners had been coming and approving the permits and making sure everything was to code. I remembered something about that from when Daddy had the upstairs put on the house and found it all very interesting. After lunch our job was to get as much painting done as we could on the walls that had been finished. The men and some of the women would finish shingling the roof. Once that was done they could do the rest of the inside work with the next group that was coming to help. The hope was to be completely back in business within a month or two. Two bathrooms needed to be repaired and three rooms they used for classes had to be replaced. The big job was the community center and I must say that watching what had transpired gave me a good feeling inside. We were all

You're Welcome

proud of what we did. I hadn't looked forward to this part of our confirmation training, but now I'm glad they required it. I met some nice people and hopefully a few friends that I could be pen pals with. After supper we took a drive around to the other side of the lake to watch the sun set. It was even more spectacular than the sunrise.

On the last morning we ate at the mess hall and then headed back home. I used the drive back to finish the list of questions that I had to answer as part of the mission's lesson. I also had to be prepared when I got back to explain everything to our class. Sam had to do that when her family went to plant indoor gardens as part of their mission to an Indian tribe in Montana. The closer we got, the more anxious I was to be home again. Four days this trip seemed like a very long time. I was glad we got back in time for me to eat with my family. That way I could tell everyone, everything at once and not have to repeat it over and over. I was in bed by seven o'clock. After all, I had school the next day.

During the next week, on Thursday night, we had our Spring Choral. The auditorium was filled with parents and grandparents that wished to hear someone they knew sing. Dad brought a few of the kids to hear me in the triple trio, which went well and I had a feeling we would be going to competition. Dad even gave me a small bouquet of flowers that he picked from the basement garden Mom kept during the winter. We would find out how we did during our chorus class sometime next week.

I babysat a few times for the two girls next door and before I knew it, the weekend was here.

On Sunday James got selected to yell surprise to me when he got up. I still wasn't too old to get a basket and even though I still had some stuff left from the basket I got as a prize, I had been looking forward to the one that would be hidden

You're Welcome

somewhere in the house and was glad I didn't miss it. Mom and Dad had postponed Easter supper and the Easter basket hunt for everyone since I was away. They all agreed to wait. I couldn't believe they did that for me. I hadn't even realized before now that we had meatloaf for supper last week not a holiday meal.

The older I got the harder it was to find my basket. It was good fun though. I found Margaret's basket before she did but didn't tell her where. The twins found theirs first. I was third to last to find mine at the very back of the linen closet.

We even got all decked out for church that day. The weather had been fairly good the past week so people were wearing light jackets and coats instead of bulky heavy ones. My coat was white with gold buttons and my Easter bonnet was lavender. Quite a sight when I think about it. I was strutting around like I was some New York model or some hot shot celebrity. I could barely see where I was walking; the brim of the hat was so wide.

S. M. Anker

After church we went straight home. Our late Easter supper would be at one o'clock on the dot. For most of our big holiday meals, I could tell you the menu by heart. I loved when Mom made her green bean dish. Not the typical one with mushroom gravy. The rest of the meal had to be ready to serve first. Then she would take a stick of butter and melt it in a skillet and when it was hot she took a couple of packages of saltine crackers and crushed them up, but not into too small of pieces. Stirring them into the butter she would brown the crackers until they would get crispy. She would mix them into the steaming hot green beans and that was it. They had to be served right away before they had a chance to get soft. They were so good. It was my turn to wash dishes, so I started and before I knew it they were all dried and put away.

My father brought out the Buttons game and I played but dropped out when Mom asked me to play the piano for her. I had finished learning a new song for my lesson and she would ask me to play it

You're Welcome

over and over. I didn't mind though because I loved playing for her. After about two hours of practice she said "Thanks Sas." and I said, "You're welcome."

Oh heck, I had wanted to go upstairs to lie down for a bit, but my tummy was off to the races, sick, sick, sick. I quickly glanced around at the clock and it was five fifteen and could not believe what I saw. When I practice the piano I usually use an old metronome that my dad had given me. It belonged to my grandfather when he was little. I was a baby when he went to be with Jesus, but I loved that I had something of his. It was pulsating like crazy now and I could not imagine how that was going to work. I ran and got my backpack from under the stairs. Mom was still sitting in her chair doing the cross-stitch piece she was working on. She didn't notice that I left and came back into the room. I sat down on the piano bench and reached my finger up to stop the pendulum which was glowing and immediately felt the room spinning. As my finger dropped to the top of the piano, my head fell a bit backwards and it felt as if I were floating on a cloud in the sky. I had to keep my eyes closed so I wouldn't feel dizzy. It lasted about a minute and when I opened my eyes I was sitting in the red velvet seat of a horse and buggy carriage. I think I was downtown.

I wasn't alone. In the seat across from me were a man and women with a small boy between them. On my seat was an older boy, maybe fifteen, and a little girl about seven. They were laughing and pointing to things as they rode by them and it was obvious they were having a good time. The small boy seemed to know I was there. He looked around two.

The cloppity clop, clop, cloppity clop, clop, of the horse's hoofs against the pavement rhythmically blended with the sounds of people moving about. After about an hour, the buggy driver pulled into an area reserved for passengers to get off. It was still early so I decided to see

You're Welcome

what they were going to do next. The young girl asked, "Are we going now, or do we still have to wait?" The man, her father no doubt, replied after looking at his watch, "No, it will be open by the time we get there." The girl seemed satisfied with that answer and I walked with them down the street.

Ten blocks later we turned the corner and we were standing in front of the Boston Store marquee. I hadn't been on this side of downtown when I was here in November, so I followed them inside. For some reason it was open at this time of day on a Sunday and we went to an elevator and didn't go up. We were headed to the basement. When the door opened there were Easter rabbits there to guide us down a slightly lit corridor. There was a very long line of people waiting for something. I saw the man take his wallet out to get some money, so I checked my pockets since I didn't get a chance to go back to get my pillow and money after I left the real world.

S. M. Anker

As we got closer I could see a sign that read; 'Adults Free, Children Two Dollars.' How ridiculous is that? Why would only children have to pay? Adults are the ones with the money. I didn't get it, but I took out two singles. As the children gave up their money I set mine down too. The cashier didn't notice mine but took it anyway. Each child was given a ticket and the parents got the other half that had been torn from the children. I saw those tickets used once at a cake raffle during the Valentine's Day Bazaar at our church. The children were guided into one door while the adults went through a different door. I followed the children.

From the moment I entered what had to be the biggest basement I ever saw, I was fascinated. The sign said 'Egg Land' across the area I was walking through. This was the last weekend it would be open from what I overheard. I could not believe my eyes. Every single thing I saw, including the floor was completely made out of Legos. There had to be gad zillions

You're Welcome

of them. First of all, as I walked into the area each section of Legos had a different colored floor. As I walked they lit up from underneath and created a path for me to walk on.

The entire basement of the department store had been turned into a Lego Easter city. They wanted us to touch everything. Not take it apart, but pick it up, move it, look at it, marvel in it. We had paid to be able to explore the city without an adult telling us not to touch anything. I thought that was cool.

We were given an Easter basket to carry and I had to pick a color and follow that path around. We were told as we began that when we got to the end of it, I had to take a brick that matched the color of the path I finished and put it in my basket. Then I needed to switch to a different color path until all six color choices were in my basket. That way I would know that I explored everything I needed to and had seen everything there was to see.

S. M. Anker

I chose the red path first. The older boy from the carriage and the two year old took the blue path. I didn't see which way the little girl went until I saw her in front of me.

The path led me into an area that had rides built out of these little molded shapes. There was a big Ferris wheel, a merry-go-round, an enormous slide and swings. I saw a girl about my size getting off the Ferris wheel, so I climbed on when the seat opened. If it held her it should hold me. I didn't even know if I weighed anything in this altered realm. I'd have to check that out at some point. Along the path there were other things to look at.

Not being keen on swings, I chose the merry-go-round next. It was so much fun and the animals looked almost real except they were hard, glossy, and didn't move. Wait, I take that back, the giraffe moved. They must have put some type of motor contraption inside it to make its neck and head move.

You're Welcome

The blue path took me to an oversized Easter basket and all the goodies inside. It was so big I could actually climb up into it and there was still enough room for at least six dozen more children. Each piece of candy or toy in the basket was made with the little bricks as well as the basket. It had a huge handle on the basket and if you pulled on the cord running down the side of the handle, you could hoist yourself right out of the basket and back to the floor. It was so much fun. I did that about five times. The yellow path led me to a small, slightly larger-than-miniature version of the Chicago skyline. It was almost like being there again. It even had a small replica of the building where I left all the pillows. Next was the green path. Along this path they had created hundreds of different kinds of flowers, bushes, and trees in a park like setting. There were benches where you could sit and admire the flowers. The people who put this display together had to be so creative. I was going to remember this when I was older. If I had Lego flowers I would never have to water them and they couldn't die. I am aware, because I'm twelve, how many man hours it took to do all of it, but to that little seven-year-old I was following, it was magical. Ellen and James would have liked it too. Funny, I found myself missing them.

The purple path let you experience a short gondola ride in Venice, Italy. I liked this path the best of them all. I might go there someday to make the comparison. The last path was pink and it took us to an area where we actually got to create a design ourselves. There were technicians and artists available to help us draw something and then actually build it. We were told to use our imaginations and create anything we wanted. All I could come up with was a hot air balloon and since I was on my own it took a while. By the time the other kids were done with their projects, I had something that resembled one. As we walked out of the room, numbers were being called and adults came up to the attendants with whatever tickets they had to collect their

You're Welcome

children. Once united they could go into another separate room and get treats for their baskets and pick up a gift to take home. I didn't have an adult so I kept my hot air balloon. No one would ever see it, but I'd remember where it came from if it didn't disappear. I wondered if it would.

While I was holding on to it though, it started pulsating and it was clear it was time to return home. I went and got my backpack from behind a table where I had stashed it and put my finger into the small basket which was glowing. I felt myself whisked up and away and was now sailing across the sky in my lopsided hot air balloon. I was surprised it even stayed up. The night was clear and the ride was unforgettable.

The balloon set me down gently on the parking lot near the Water Fall. I didn't leave the altered realm until I stepped onto the ground. I was fairly comfortable until then and now I was cold. I walked in the backdoor, up to my room, got my pajamas on, went back downstairs, gave both my parents a kiss and told them goodnight and I went to bed. I even stopped in and gave James, Margaret, Victoria and Ellen a cheek kiss. They were already asleep. Amelia and Helene were still up so we talked for a while and then we all went to bed at the same time.

The next day we were off school because of an unexpected snow storm. Sam called me around ten and asked me to come over. She told me about getting a new bedroom set, complete with new linen, a bedspread, pillows and curtains. Her older sister was graduating and would be going off to college and the upstairs bedroom would be all hers. I could tell she was a little excited.

Once I had finished my bedroom chores; ironing all the pillowcases, handkerchiefs, and my dad's work shirts, and dusting the top of the refrigerator, Mom said I could go until supper time. I took a couple of my new forty-fives with me to play on her record player. We listened to music and talked all afternoon. I gave her more details about the mission trip and told her

You're Welcome

all about the most recent trip. We were making plans to hang out the next day if we were off school again and her Mom asked if I wanted to stay there to eat and then sleep over.

I called my Mom from the downstairs phone and she said it was okay, but not to stay away all day tomorrow if we were off and to come home right after school if we went. Sam's dad said he would drop me at my bus stop if we did. She also wanted me to come home and pack a bag to take back with my pajamas and my toothbrush. When I got home and got the bag together, she handed me another one full of homemade donuts to take to Sam's mother for dessert. I kissed her on the cheek and told her I loved her and thanked her for letting me spend the night. She said, "You're welcome." I heard Arthur and Richard giggling from all the way up in their room.

Chapter Fifteen

Before doing anything else, we went up to her bedroom. Her sister's stuff was still there but moved toward the other side of the room. Her new double bed was pretty with the new bedspread and it matched the curtains around the window. She showed me the inside of her dresser drawers and how the bed was on a frame with four drawers underneath it for even more storage. We put my stuff away and headed to the basement.

The renovations being done before her birthday party, next week, were almost finished and we were going to help paint. The carpenters had completed a bar on the other end of the long space and had finished painting the ceiling. They wanted that done before we painted the walls and they put the paneling around the bar and glued down the countertop. Her mother had gone to the hardware store and picked out a sandy beige color that would look nice against the paneling they had installed. Sam got to pick out the accent color which was a shade of orange, only it looked more like fire.

We painted for about two hours and had to let everything dry before seeing if it needed another coat. When we finished with supper we checked it and it seemed okay. Sam thought it looked nice and I thought the orange lines gave it personality. The carpenters even made a little stage for the band to play on. There was still a little beige paint left so we painted the stage too. We went back upstairs because they were going to put in the new tile floor and we would be in the way. We played some records and talked. Her mom made some popcorn for us and then when it was time to go to bed she yelled up that we didn't have school the next day either.

After breakfast in the morning, which consisted of the rest of the doughnuts warmed up, eggs sunny side up, and bacon, we went downstairs and used the burnt orange paint to create flowers and put little peace symbols all over the stage.

S. M. Anker

When that paint dried we put a spot of beige paint in the middle of each flower. It reminded us of a van we had seen at the park one day that was owned by hippies. Sam thought the stage looked fantastic. I went to the store with the family to get a few things and when we got back headed home. I didn't see Sam again until the day of her party. I did find out when I went back to school that the Triple Trio was selected to go to the State competitions.

Sam's birthday fell on a Saturday and with no school the next day most of the people invited had responded that they would be there. Her mother had let her invite about thirty friends to help her celebrate becoming a teenager.

The party was starting at six o'clock that evening and I went over early to help her decorate. She and I blew up about one hundred balloons and taped them all over the room. We also hung some gold streamers that were left over from New Year's Eve. The place looked so cool.

You're Welcome

There was one table set up in the corner for presents and I put mine there first. I had gotten her a silver identification bracelet with her name engraved on it. I had checked with her mother first because they were very popular, and I didn't want to do it if she had already gotten her one. She hadn't, so it was my first grown up gift to her. I had bought it months ago on one of our trips to Packard Mills. I also made her a card. I signed it "Best wishes for a great year of fun adventures."

The rest of the band arrived about an hour early and we all set up the equipment. I tested the drums and the microphones to make sure they were working. Her father had to adjust the loudness of the amplifiers though. He didn't want the neighbors complaining.

Her guests started to arrive about quarter to six. It was my job to take their coats and put them on the rack that her mother had emptied in the basement laundry room. When you came down the stairs, if you turned left, you walked into the renovated part of the basement. If you turned right, you walked into the laundry area. There was a door on it that kept people from looking in. Her father had set up this rack using the handle of an old broom and some wood things that came down from the overhead beams. The two wood things had holes in them that fit the size of the broom handle. It made a great place for storing their winter coats and clothes during the summer. Tonight, it was being used for Sam's guests.

I would take their coat and walk them down the steps and direct them into the party and go hang their coat up before going back upstairs. Sam spent her time getting birthday wishes and greeting everyone that came. My legs got tired from going up and down the stairs. When all the guests were accounted for, I went into the party. Her birthday present table was so full I needed to rearrange them so they wouldn't accidently fall off. We started playing background music at a volume you could talk over. Later on we would be able to turn it up to the volume her father had approved.

You're Welcome

Everyone was dancing and having a good time. Nearly an hour went by and Sam asked everyone to go upstairs to the living room. While there, the tables downstairs were transformed into a buffet line with the food Sam's mother had made. There was a large kettle of Sloppy Joes, a tray of hamburger buns, a vegetable tray, cherry Jell-O, potato salad, chips and dip, and pretzels. At one end of the table there were paper plates, napkins and plastic forks and spoons. When everything was set up the guests were invited to come back downstairs.

At the other end of the table on a wooden box was a big wash bin that was full of ice. Inside the bin were bottles of soda from the local B&B Soda Company. Sam's father had a bottle opener attached on the wall which made it easy. You could do it one handed while you held your plate. The cap would fall into the bin he had put under it. Clink, clink, is the sound it made all night long. In addition to liking the orange soda, I also drank some of the cream soda.

S. M. Anker

Everyone got enough to eat and then some. When everyone was done, Sam's older sister brought down her birthday cake. It was a sheet cake which is exactly how it sounds. Like a sheet of cake. One layer of thin chocolate cake about two inches high in a rectangle about three feet by two foot. The top of it was decorated in vanilla almond butter frosting with Pink letters spelling out the words "Happy Birthday Teenager," with little rosettes all about. Thirteen little yellow candle holders held the lit candles. The guitar player played 'Happy Birthday' as we all sang to her and she made her wish and blew out all the candles at once.

They didn't cut the cake right away though. It was time for her to open the presents. She got a ton of good stuff. My gift had been pushed to the back of the table so was one of the last ones to be opened. She liked it.

After that we put records on instead of playing and got to dance. Her sister cut the cake into pieces and put them on small

You're Welcome

paper plates and walked around the room with them. Everyone took a piece and before you knew it, it was gone. Neither of us got a piece. The party ended around nine thirty and by ten everyone was gone. Mom had let me spend the night again, so I didn't have to go anywhere. As we were going upstairs her mother handed us each a huge frosted cupcake that she had made extra and set aside. We talked half the night away and finally fell asleep around three in the morning with a gentle nudge from Sam's father.

Chapter Sixteen

The rest of the month went by quickly. Most of the snow was gone and the stores all had summer clothes in them. I only saw Sam occasionally. I was busy after school two nights practicing for the State competitions in May and I still had my piano lessons on Saturdays. I had also landed a spot on the High School Summer Swim Team so had to go there to practice once a week.

I had intended to tell Sam that I was working on a surprise for her but it was going to take a little longer. I wanted to test a few more things in the altered realm first before I could decide. Some of it was still very confusing and I wouldn't do it unless I was sure. Mom called up the stairs to see if I would go to the store for her. She needed milk before supper.

I said "Sure, no problem."
"Thanks, Sas."
"You're welcome."

You're Welcome

Oh buggers, I was always amazed at how fast that happened. I did feel sick but didn't see anything pulsating or spinning or glowing so maybe I wasn't going anywhere. Or maybe there were two dogs running around trying to get in. Or three fish? I started laughing to myself and had a terrible time getting my shoes on. When I did I went downstairs and by this time Mom had a list made out.

"Thought you needed milk?"

"Well, as long as you were going I thought I'd have you pick up a few more things." she replied.

"Okay." I said. She handed me the money and I was off to the store. When I got there I grabbed a cart. I liked pushing it fast and jumping on the edge and coasting until it stopped or hit something. This time the something was the display of mustard. I picked up as many as I could and then told one of the clerks. It didn't look as bad when he came over and no glass bottles broke. He said not to worry about it. "Stuff like this happens all the time." Whew, that was close.

I got everything on Mom's list without another incident and 'accidently on purpose' left money for the trouble the clerk had putting the display back together. While I was walking home I could see my house. The chimney on the roof was glowing. Really?

I put the groceries away and went to get my stuff. I grabbed a few cases out of the linen closet. I had already repacked the backpack after the last trip, but Mom had Oreo cookies on the shopping list. I took a few out of the cookie jar. I was already hungry and was going to miss supper tonight. I didn't know where I would end up once I climbed up on the roof, so I also took an apple on the way out. The roof was much steeper than I thought it was. Good thing I didn't have to worry about a clumsy coat getting in the way. It was supposed to rain later tonight but that didn't seem to pose a problem either.

First thing I did was toss my stuff up on the roof. Next, I climbed up the swing set

You're Welcome

which was close to the rain drain by my parent's bedroom. I barely made the catch but was able to manage to slide one leg up the part of the roof covering the back hall. Once I was there the rest was easy. I had watched the old roofers walk up there when they were building the upstairs and they were very confident like they knew they were not going to fall off or into the roof. I copied them. I walked very straight and confident and, in a few steps, made it with my stuff to the chimney. When I got close enough to it, I could see that it was pulsating, so I climbed up a bit and put my hand and half my arm inside. I was off. Not like before when it felt like I was moving.

I was off the roof. I was standing in front of a pane of glass watching a bunch of people watching a bunch of babies. I was in a hospital. I walked around and found an atrium near the center of the hospital and went in and sat down. Why had I come to this place? There must be a reason. I hadn't known anyone recently going into the hospital except that lady

S. M. Anker

Barb's husband Bill who got hurt at work. This wasn't the same one he was in. I wondered if maybe he was there anyway, so I went to the visitor's desk and looked at the roster the clerk was referring to when talking with someone. I couldn't read it, so I grabbed it when she set it down and a copy came easily into my hand.

I looked through the whole list and there was someone there with the first name William. I went to check to see if it was him. The William on the list was in room one sixty-eight on the West wing. When I got there, Barb was sitting in the chair. Bill was in the bed with his arm hanging in this contraption from the frame of the bed. He didn't look well. I hung around to see if I could figure out why he was there and found out that when he broke his arm earlier in the year at work it never healed properly. He had to come to the hospital here to see a specialist. They decided they would have to break his arm and re-set it and they had to put a pin or something in the arm. He seemed to be

You're Welcome

fine, but Barb, she was a different story. Scatterbrained is what Daddy would have called it. I heard her complaining to someone on the phone how she wished she could be in two places at one time. I laughed, because I knew I was. They seemed okay. I walked back to the maternity ward window where I was when I first got there.

I was watching babies for a reason. I knew it. I was able to walk into the nursery where I washed my hands before touching any of them. They seemed to sense me there. I saw a little boy baby, who was crying, whose name was Baby Boy something. Then I noticed many of the baby's name cards said that. So why didn't these little human beings have names yet? I mean really, my Mom had nine months to decide on what to call her children. I would have to ask her if I was ever just Baby Girl.

This was as good a place as any, if not better than any place I could come up with, to test my theories. I already knew that money I took with me into the altered realm could not be seen by anyone but if I went back for it afterwards I could use it to pay for things if I simply held onto it until I put it down for that intention. People could see the money. I also knew if I picked up a bottle of shampoo in the altered realm that I hadn't brought with me, when I put it down there would be two bottles of shampoo and in the real world they could see two bottles.

However, if I brought a bottle with me into the altered realm, there would be one bottle and the people in the real world could not see it. Same with my clothes and anything else I brought. That's why I went back for my pillow. I also knew if I picked up a phone receiver that was attached to a stationery phone base that if I didn't move the base or pick it up, when I put the receiver down, there would be only one phone. *'What if I could bring something alive into the altered realm with me and leave with it'?*

I had decided to test that out. **B**efore I touched the chimney, I picked up a small bug and put it in a jar and carried it with

You're Welcome

me into the altered realm. I put it out on the counter in the baby nursery right next to one of the nurses' cup of coffee. She about near had a fit when she saw it squirming around.

So, if I bring it in with me and I'm not holding it she could see it, unlike the money. Once I put it back in the jar and had my hand on it she couldn't see it anymore and she looked to find it. So that was altogether different. If it wasn't dead when I got back that meant that I could take a living thing into the altered realm and safely return it. How to bring it into the altered realm without someone seeing it or explain its absence would be the problem to solve and focus on.

To test the other theory, I needed to already be in the altered realm. Since I was, I picked up one of the babies like I had with the dog in the park. The baby was in my arms and was also still in the crib in the nursery. However, no one could see me or the baby. I realized that I had no way of finding out what happened to those fish or dogs in the altered world and was worried about the baby that replicated. This woman didn't have twins and she would never see the other one. What would happen to it? I laid the baby back in its crib alongside the other baby boy and nothing seemed out of place. I could see two of them, but the nurse picked up only one and the other was still there. It was like me crawling into bed with myself already there. I hadn't felt my body when I laid down. It hit me then, I did have a way of checking. I had to, right now, get to the Dairy Dutch to see how many fish were in the tank. I knew that night Sam only saw fourteen but would there still be seventeen fish swimming in the tank in the altered realm?

I went to the front registration desk and looked for something to tell me where the hospital was. At least I knew the name of the city and the direction I needed to head. I geared up and began to space run southeast. About an hour later I had gone far enough to see things that were familiar to me. I wasn't even tired from the run. Another fifteen minutes and I was

You're Welcome

standing in the parking lot. I went inside directly to the fish tank and counted fourteen fish. That meant when I go back from this realm, the things I have replicated disappear. That is all I needed to know. The extra shampoo, the clothes, the girl's car keys, all would have disappeared. The baby would too.

In the blink of an eye I realized I could help Barb. If I replicated her she would be in the altered realm and I could explain it to her. She could get everything done that she needed to and still be there to take care of Bill and Jean Rae. So, after getting a burger that had been delivered to table seven and an order of onion rings from table three, I left some money at the cashier's and was off back to the hospital. I went straight to Bill's room and as Barb was standing near his bed, I grabbed her as hard as I could around the legs and hoisted her up with all the strength I could muster.

I don't know what I was expecting, but as one Barb fell forward on top of Bill's bed, another Barb fell backwards into this big monitoring thing and a bunch of sirens started blaring. She was the one in the real world. In less than twenty seconds, a nurse and two attendants were in the room checking the monitor to see what was wrong. Barb in the real world was standing there watching and telling Bill that it was probably a glitch in some circuit or other. Barb in the altered realm picked herself off the bed and looking me square in the face, asked "What the heck is happening here?"

"Can you see and hear me then?" I asked her.

"Of course, I can see you and hear you. The problem is I can see me over there standing by Bill, as well."

I told her I could explain all of that and asked her to come with me and not worry about Bill because she was still going to be there with him. I could tell she was confused. Most of the time I was confused by what was happening. I had to coax her, but we walked down to the atrium and sat down. I explained everything that was happening to me on these adventures

You're Welcome

and that I had heard her earlier telling someone how she had wished there were two of her. I told her I had made that happen.

"I don't believe you." she said. I asked her to think back to last November for a minute. "By any chance, did you notice anything peculiar at your house?"

"Like what?" she asked.

"Like maybe one day you walked into the bathroom and you couldn't quite figure out where the extra five bars of soap came from, or three extra towels."

"Or why I had three bottles of my favorite expensive shampoo for a day that later vanished?" she said,

"Yeah, like that." I said to her.

I told her that if she called up into Bill's room and asked to talk to Barb, she would come on the phone, so she called but I made sure the phone base was stationery. I had told her that I wasn't sure who would end up with the memory of this because it was the first time trying it. When the other Barb came to the phone, this Barb told her not to worry about anything because everything that she needed to get done would get done. I heard her say that her prayer had been answered. I wasn't answering anyone's prayer, which was God's job, I only wanted to help.

Then she told herself something, that only she knew, to prove that she was telling herself the truth and that they had a new friend, me, that was helping. Barb in the alternate realm said she wasn't sure why she was trusting me, but if all this was going to work, she needed her purse. The other Barb would also need it, so I went back to the room and picked Barb's purse up leaving it there with her and taking it with me. To ease Barb's mind in the altered realm, she had to call back and ask herself if she still had her purse. She did so she said, "What's next?"

I told her she could go home and do everything she needed to and not to worry about taking care of the baby or Bill. Her other self would do that. I explained that I had no way of knowing what her other

You're Welcome

self would do in the real world while she was running errands in the altered realm and that some chores could overlap so she made another call to the other Barb to make sure she focused on Bill and the baby.

I let her know that I wouldn't be going home for a few days to give her enough time and that I'd probably spend the night in Bill's room. "You will not!" she said. "You will come home with me. I have a spare room you can use, and if you happen to quadruple the amount of shampoo I have, I won't be sorry." I laughed and so did she, but I reminded her we had to use this gift in the right way. I thought helping her was the right thing.

The next few days I saw very little of Barb. She was doing all the things she needed to and getting more done than she ever thought possible. When she came home to 'check-up' on me she would cook me a meal if I was hungry. Once when she came back I had made a pizza that I

S. M. Anker

found in the freezer. When she was feeling confident that she could spend time with Bill at the hospital and not worry about anything else she asked how she got back. I explained that when I went back to my real world she in this altered realm should disappear, but I didn't know when. I needed to know after that happened if she retained all the memories of me. I asked her to give me her phone number. I would wait a few hours to leave the altered realm, then I would call her. I told her I would say "This is Sas calling to see how Bill is doing." She would need to say; 'Purple socks', back to me so that I knew she was back in the real world. If she knew what to say, then I would know that she also remembered everything and that the other Barb would already be gone. "I'd also like you to write down the date and time of the exact moment when you remember everything as Barb in the real world and the words purple socks." She said she would. After saying goodbye one last time, I headed home.

You're Welcome

As I got to the backyard, I glanced up at the roof, nope not there. I looked around the backyard and the door on the outside shed was pulsating and the door handle had a faint glow. I waited exactly two hours to walk over and open the door, right into my next class. I was at school. I glanced at my watch and it was eleven twenty-eight on Monday, April twenty-seventh. I wrote it down.

Chapter Seventeen

I waited until Wednesday to contact Barb. When I did she could hardly wait for me to tell her who I was or why I was calling. She kept saying "Purple socks, purple socks." I yelled into the phone for her to stop, told her it was me and asked how she was doing.

"I'm doing great, feel fine, remember everything, and I can't find another Barb around anywhere. I also wrote down that I remembered everything on Monday at eleven-thirty in the morning." I told her that my watch said eleven twenty-eight when I got back, but we didn't synchronize them before I left so that was close enough for me.

She said there was no pain or awareness of leaving the altered realm, she was back in the real world again. "I was actually feeding Jean Rae when I got back so I'm guessing that was what I was doing when I came back. I also could only find the purse I had with me in the real world, but it now had the notes and things

You're Welcome

I put in it from the altered realm. I told her that was new. Since I hadn't replicated anyone before I didn't know how that would work and it was good to know. It was also good to know when I go back to the real world, everything I create in the altered realm disappears immediately and that the real person remembers everything. I wondered if she would remember everything in the future. We talked about how Bill was doing and when he would be coming home.

Since Barb didn't live too far away and she was on my bus route, we made plans to see each other again. Maybe next month, if I would like to, she would take me with her to the zoo when she took Jean Rae. I told her that maybe she would want to jot down somewhere what happened to her and hide it away, in case someday the memory was gone.

I gave her my full name, address, and phone number to write down. If she ever found the note about these events and she had no memory of it, she should put in her note to call me and I would explain.

I was going to embark on a relationship with her in the real world that would filter into the altered realm. Maybe she would be willing to test my picture theory out. Bill would never believe her, so she said nothing at all to him for the time being. She only told him that I was someone that might be babysitting for Jean Rae. She wasn't lying.

I only saw Sam a few times in the first two weeks of May. I told her some of what had happened, but not everything about Barb. I would do that later.

At the end of the second week of May we had our State competitions. We had practiced so much we were anxious to get to the university, about one hundred and fifty miles northwest of us, and get it over with. There were other small ensembles from a few middle schools going and we would all be judged together in one group. However, no other triple trio was going from any other middle or elementary

You're Welcome

school. I was proud of that. I had worked hard to get in the group during auditions.

Saturday, we had to be at the high school by seven o'clock in the morning for check in. Buses had been rented to take us to the university and would be leaving promptly at seven-thirty. The choir director said that if any choir member was late and missed the bus, they had to get there on their own power. If they didn't get there in time, they got an 'F' for the semester. I would remember that if she was still the director when I got to tenth grade. Our music teacher only told us that if one of us didn't show up, the triple trio would not perform. We all knew how important it was and showed up by seven. I was grateful that I had gone to the altered realm already in the past month, so I would be there for the experience.

We got to sit together in one of the buses that had the madrigal group from the choir. We both sang for each other the pieces of music we would be performing because both groups would be singing at two forty-five in the afternoon and we wouldn't be able to sit in on each other's competitions.

There were nine sites around the university where students performed (rooms one to five were for instrumental and six to nine were for vocals). Parents, friends, and all the other spectators were free to watch performances throughout the day. We could also listen to anyone we wanted prior to or after we performed. Of course, I went to listen to the senior high choir, but I also heard some choirs from other parts of the state that were very good. Afterwards I went to hear some of the instrumental ensembles and some drum and piano solos. There were many smaller groups that sang, but not that many triple trios. I counted about sixteen from other areas and listened to about ten of them. They were good, but I hoped the judges thought our group was better.

About a half hour before we were scheduled to sing our music teacher had instructed us to find the room we would be performing in and get together and do vocal warming up. We were doing that when she showed up. She was very nervous for some reason, which made me very nervous. She kept saying there was nothing to be nervous about, but I could see her hands shaking. How was she going to hold the baton if she was shaking so badly?

There was a great deal of pressure on her. Most of the high school groups had to compete at the District level first. If they received a 'first or superior' rating from the judges, then they were invited to move on to the statewide competitions. We had not competed at the District level. We had been personally invited by a few of the judges that had been at District and were visiting schools around the state looking for a school ensemble they believed deserved to be at State but couldn't because it was for high schools only. I guess when I think about it, that is a lot of pressure.

I sometimes felt that pressure at home. I started taking care of my little brother and sisters when I was only about seven years old. I was always the big sister. Sometimes I resent having to spend so much time with them now because of it. The feeling was stronger than it is now though. Somehow being away from the family in the altered realm was helping. Richard, Arthur and Amelia had to watch me and Helene quite a bit when we were younger, and I wondered if they resented me for it. I'd have to keep that in mind when I was being snippy to them in the future. I guess that is what being a family is all about.

When we heard the call for our group, we approached the judges. We had to introduce ourselves and hand them a copy of the sheet music we had chosen to sing. Once that was done we were directed to the stage. The judges cued the music teacher as to when to begin. She never did until she had all of us looking at her at the same time. She tipped her baton and the piano started to play. I can only say that I don't ever remember sounding so good.

You're Welcome

The notes were perfectly pitched and not one person messed up.

When we were done, everyone in the auditorium was clapping for us. It was wonderful. For a few minutes the judges were talking among themselves and one asked for a recess of ten minutes. Our music teacher let some of us run to the bathroom but had everyone else run vocal warm-ups, so we would be ready when the judge came back. After the break, when we returned inside, the auditorium was completely filled. There were even people standing in the back area that didn't have seats. We didn't know what happened, but we all felt even more pressure going into the next number.

Our teacher tipped her baton once more, the piano started to play, and we were into our second number. The richness of the notes was never better. The acoustics in the auditorium made us sound like we were at Carnegie Hall. The audience must have thought so too because the applause we got was immeasurable. It took a while, but we completed our final piece and the audience was on their feet. Was the standing ovation for us? The music teacher tipped her baton and in unison we all took a bow. Then she took one. She had the biggest smile on her face that I ever saw. We were excused then to visit other groups singing but we had to be at the bus area by four-thirty at the latest.

Buses were scheduled to leave promptly at five. We wouldn't find out until next week what the judges thought and how they scored us. I went off to find a group to listen to. I was pretty hungry, but it had been pre-scheduled for us to stop on the way home and get something. I did find a reception area that had some small cucumber sandwiches, so I had three or four. I only listened to two other groups before heading to the bus area at four-fifteen. I stopped at the bathroom first and overheard someone say, "Did you hear the elementary school that sang this afternoon?"

"No, I was listening to my brother's trumpet solo, what happened?"

You're Welcome

"Well, from what I gather the judge had to stop the show for about ten minutes."

"Why?" the girl asked.

"She went into the halls and told everyone she saw that if they wanted to hear something fantastic they needed to go to the auditorium and listen to the school that was performing, so I went, and they were very good."

I caught myself smiling so hard my cheeks hurt. The judge liked us. I knew I wanted to be in choir when I got to high school. I had to run to get to the bus area on time.

The end of the following week came quickly. Sometime during our first class, the principle made his usually boring announcements.

"Well, good morning students and teachers, and happy Thursday. I have a few reminders for you. There is baseball practice for squads Red and Blue immediately after school. Suit up and meet your coach on the field by three thirty. Also, for those of you on the debate team, your meeting during sixth period today is cancelled. A makeup session will be held next Monday during seventh period.

Now, I will read the names of the students who represented our school last Saturday at the State competitions." He read off mine and the names of the other eight members. "It is with great pride that I tell you that they have received an 'A' rating or 'First' from the panel of judges. A superior rating is given to only the very best." I couldn't contain myself and let out a holler. The entire homeroom was clapping for me. "The judges also wanted you to know that no other entry from an elementary school received a rating that high, so good job girls." I was beside myself silly with the news. We had music class after homeroom and all of us were comparing what the experience was like and who said what, when they were being congratulated.

I called Sam when I got home from school and she said, "I knew you would get a superior rating." I told her what the music teacher said about getting a trophy before school was out and I did get a medal that I would show her later.

When I got off the bus after school the next day and headed to the house I saw something that startled me. The house next door to me was above the ground on a huge platform of wood. I had almost forgotten that they were going to move it.

The family had moved two months ago into a new home in the city next to ours. I have visited them several times, but they kept putting off moving the house because of zoning laws or something like that. Now the house was going to move. When I got home I asked Mom how long it was going to take, and she said it would be done Saturday. I called Sam and asked her if she wanted to watch it Saturday. If we hung out at the park we could see it when it turned the corner and watch it until it got to the yard it was going on. It's a very weird thing to see a big house moving down the road like a car.

S. M. Anker

'I have to chuckle when I think of the weird stuff going on in my life at the moment'.

Saturday, I didn't get away from taking the twins with me and we stayed in the park most of the afternoon until it was time to eat. The house had gotten all the way down the block and made the second turn by the time we left. Sam and I were going to see if our parents would let us come back after supper. Not everyone gets to see something like this. Even the people who lived on the blocks the house was passing were sitting in their lawn chairs watching the progress from their front yards. After supper we met back up to watch for a while, but I had to take Helene with me and had an eight o'clock curfew. With the street lights on it was an eerie sight, this house, rolling along ever so slowly. Before we left for home, around quarter to eight, they had gotten it to the lot. We had to watch more the next day and then after the house was in place we focused our time waiting for the new bank to start building. I would be able to

You're Welcome

watch out the bathroom window anytime I wanted. However, we didn't know when that would start.

I hadn't talked to Barb in a couple of weeks, so I called to see how her husband was. I also asked about Jean Rae. Barb told me that she would be turning one year old later in the month and she was planning a little party for her. Her grandparents and a few aunts and uncles and cousins would be there.

"You are more than welcome to join us." She told me. "I think of you as Jean Rae's older sister." I was thinking to myself that I wanted to say to her, that I didn't need another little sister, I had quite enough of my own. Instead, I told her I would have to ask my Mom, but it sounded like fun. I did like Jean Rae and Ellen was getting older now. On Monday, she sent me an invitation in the mail for the party. When my mom saw it she asked me who she was. I told her that I had met her on the bus, she was the driver, and that she lived somewhere downtown and that we had talked about me possibly babysitting for her daughter.

The party would give her a chance to see me interact with Jean Rae. I had babysat for the girls who lived next door and Mom knew I had practice being around babies, so she said if I wanted to go I could. She would have to call Barb and talk with her first. Mom called later that day and must have had a good conversation because she was letting me go. Mom got the directions to her house and she told me if my father could drive me there he would. He had been working overtime on Saturdays for about two months now. If he had to work, I could take the bus.

I would be staying overnight there to watch Jean Rae after the party, so Barb and Bill could go out to a movie. They would bring me home the next day, so they could meet each other. I told Mom that I would do anything she wanted for letting me go and she said, "That's so very sweet of you, thanks."

"You're welcome."

You're Welcome

The nausea was beginning to lessen a bit when I thought 'now what?' What on earth was I going to do? How would this work out? I got my backpack and figured I would get a message to Barb and if I replicated anything she could handle it. Somehow, I would get to her house to replicate my pillow. I looked around to see where my exit would take place. I walked around the entire house, inside and out at least three times and saw nothing. I started my fourth trip when it caught my attention. I had barely seen it at all, so I looked closer. Yup, that was for sure my exit point.

It was the mirror hanging on the wall in the main bathroom. When I looked in the mirror it had two sides that moved so that I could see all sides of what I was looking at. I used it to fix the back of my hair when I put it up. This time when I looked into the mirror there was a faint glow in the reflection coming from the bathtub. I had looked directly into the bathtub several times and did not see it pulsating, but now, looking at it in the mirror it appeared to be doing that. Question was, did I have to get into the tub from the mirror?

I remembered what happened to me when I touched the weight on the metronome. If I touched the bathtub in the mirror, then maybe I would be in the bathtub. I tried and in a second the whole room started moving. This time instead of entering somewhere immediately, it all moved rather slowly. Not like slow motion, but it seemed to take forever for me to get where I was obviously going. Then it all stopped. I never moved anywhere. I was still standing in front of the mirror with my finger on it. I still felt somewhat sick. The only way I could figure out if I was in the altered realm was to test it out. I picked up a roll of toilet paper and there was one still in the spot that I had taken it from. I stacked it on top of the one already there knowing in this house we could never have enough.

It dawned on me that I didn't have to go anywhere this trip. I could stay here.

You're Welcome

That idea got me thinking about the real world me. I knew Barb from the altered realm and while I was in the real world I knew who she was. In the altered realm, the real me, wouldn't know who Barb was and would question why she was going to a complete stranger's house to babysit a child she had never met. What if she refused to go to Barb's? Would Mom make her go saying that she had already told Barb I would be there? I decided I had to get to Barb's before the party.

I slept in my own bed Friday night and first thing Saturday I space ran to Barb's.
Once I was there I started trying to get her attention. I dropped a fork on the floor but that didn't work. I tried splashing water on her when she was running the tap. There was no recognition. I ran upstairs to Jean Rae's room and dug through her drawers until I found the perfect thing, a pair of purple socks. I grabbed them and headed back to the kitchen. I set them down on the counter where she was standing. Picked

them up and set another pair down. The fourth time I did it she said "That will be just about enough of that. How many pairs of purple socks does one little girl need?" She knew I was there.

She went and got a pad of paper and pen and I wrote what had happened explaining that I wouldn't know her when I got there. She would have to come up with something to make it all seem normal and I told her not to worry about Jean Rae, because I love babies in the real world too. I told her I wasn't going to stay because it would be too weird, but that as soon as the real me got home Sunday, I would be back if I was still in the altered realm or I would call her if I wasn't. Then I started to go home. I changed my mind though. If I went home I wouldn't have memories from Jean Rae's first birthday, and somehow that seemed important. So I went back, but I'd tell Barb later.

The house was full of people by two o'clock. It was fun watching myself interact with these strangers. Jean Rae

You're Welcome

was having as much fun as a one year old can. I believe parties like this are more for the adults to fuss over the baby. Lots of pictures were taken and I would be in some of them. I even managed to place myself in some of the pictures the real me didn't get in. I tried to remember which ones they were for us to check later on.

I was shocked that I sang Happy Birthday so well, no one else was singing. Barb stared at me and said that she didn't know I could sing and that would come in handy getting Jean Rae to bed at night. I watched Barb open a few of the presents and it hit me that the real me thought she was babysitting and wouldn't have gotten a present. I was pleasantly surprised when I did hand Barb a little box.

Inside was something called the Shape-O Ball. It was perfect for little Jean Rae. The ball had holes of different shapes cut out and Jean Rae would have to learn which holes to put the shaped blocks in. I must have gotten it from the lady who lived across the street a few doors down.

S. M. Anker

She was the only one selling Tupperware on the block.

It was a nice party, but I decided to go home. I had my memory of it and I was tired. I space ran and when I got home I went straight to the mirror to see if that is where I needed to be. It wasn't. The big tub was doing the pulsating thing. I didn't get in because I needed to stay at Barb's until Sunday when she brought me home. I didn't know if I went back now if I would stay there.

I hung out in the bedroom the rest of the weekend. I couldn't do anything I wanted because it all end up with stuff being replicated. I tried to play solitaire, but I had about a hundred cards before I decided to stop.

Sunday, I got up as usual and went to church and catechism class. I would be ahead of schedule and on the way home I walked by the house that moved and they had seeded the lawn and it looked like the lady of the house had planted some flowers. There was also a new tree in the yard. The only thing that looked out of

You're Welcome

place was the little girl playing in the driveway. She wasn't my friend.

I came home about two-thirty. The real me, was in the bedroom and I went downstairs to the bathroom. The bathtub was still pulsating, so I climbed in. As I did, I found myself bent over and wobbling on top of my mattress on the top bunk and Amelia was watching me. I attempted to jump up and down a few times and then sat down. She looked at me and said, "You know Mom doesn't like it when you do that."

I said, "I know." Then, and I don't know why, I added, "I love you sis." She looked at me like I was crazy.

Chapter Eighteen

During the next week it occurred to me that I should probably take the same advice I had given Barb. Especially remembering the conversation I had with my sister about the time I came in the milk chute, and she didn't have a clue what I was talking about. If there was the slightest chance that I wasn't going to remember any of this I would want to have it written down somewhere. I would also want to put Barb's address and phone number down because she would be doing the same with my information. If both of us had it written, then we would have to believe that it actually happened. At least that made sense to me.

I took some of my allowance and went to the dime store and bought a couple of spiral notebooks that I would record everything in. I put a large number one on the outside of the first one and started writing everything I could remember beginning with my birthday last year.

You're Welcome

Over the course of the next couple of weeks, I had filled two of the notebooks plus some in a third. I put them, for the time being, at the back of the cabinet dresser under my summer clothes. Amelia, Helene and I had always respected each other's space, so I didn't need to worry about them finding them. They would be fine there for now and I would work on coming up with a better place to keep the notebooks.

On Wednesday of the second week of June, Mom announced at breakfast before we left for school, that we shouldn't make any plans with anyone for Saturday. We were going to our Grandma's house for a family picnic as soon as my piano lesson was over. When we had a family picnic there was no excuse good enough to miss it.

I never got to know my Grandfather and Grandma got remarried two years ago and I went to the wedding. He died though, last summer. She had been by herself for a little over a year, again. She liked having these 'spur of the moment' picnics so she could see how big we were all getting. They were always fun because I got to see all my cousins on my dad's side of the family; there were ten in all unless I counted the ones that sometimes came up from Missouri which would make it nineteen, plus my aunts and uncles.

Grandma had a big old farm house with a big barn. There was a huge amount of land out back to play hide and seek and an even bigger front yard. There was privet hedge growing on either side of the sidewalk leading up to her front door. Sometimes the hedge would be trimmed into a neatly formed square and other times it was grown out wild, all over the place. I liked it all wild because it was harder to see around them when we were playing tag. When everyone got to Grandma's the rest of the front yard would be lined with all the lawn chairs everyone brought.

Sometimes it would be months before everyone got to see one another and they would spend the entire day talking about how the family had been, what was going on at work, and stuff like that. I heard Mom talking about the Easter egg contest I had won. While all this was going on, the women would also be putting the finishing touches on the food. Sometimes the men would grill hamburgers and hotdogs and sometimes Grandma put on a roast. There would always be grilled corn on the cob.

The kitchen in the house was small for a farm house. Most of the farm houses I saw on television had big kitchens, bigger than ours at home, where people sat at a huge table and there was still room to walk around. Hers wasn't designed to eat in. Along the outside wall was the sink and preparation area and the cabinets that held her dishes, silverware, and food. On the other side of the kitchen was a stove and refrigerator. In the middle of the floor was a trap door that went down into a cellar.

If I ate inside grandma's house it would be at the dining room table. However, that wouldn't have enough room for our family either, let alone the other four families.

The one thing I don't like about going to Grandma's is the house smells nasty. At any given time, there are at least ten cats somewhere in her house. That didn't include all of the ones outside in the yard, but they don't bother me out there. I usually spent as much of my visit as I could outside in the yard. When it was time to eat, we would line up in front of the kitchen, wash at the sink, and get a plate. The food was spread out on the counters and some of it was even outside on the picnic table. Once I had my food, I'd find a place to eat. Us kids let the adults have the lawn chairs and we got creative about finding our own spots. I liked eating out near the old barn. There weren't any animals out there except an occasional field mouse a cat hadn't found.

Grandpa number one had made jewelry when he was alive and tended bee hives for the honey. The old barn was filled with his tools and things. There was usually an old tractor tire or two some of

You're Welcome

us would sit on to eat. If it was a nice day, some of us would go crabbing after lunch down by the creek. If we got bored with that we would walk up to the elementary school and play on the swings or play tag in the yard.

It was usually my aunts and uncles that decided the picnic was over not Grandma. We would all give her tons of kisses and hugs before we would go. This family outing ended like they all did, at Dairy O. I had a marshmallow malt this time.

School finished in the next week and I was glad. The man who lived on the corner on the other side of the apartment building had two small girls and he and his wife wanted me to babysit for them all summer.

For some reason Mom thought this would be a good idea. I wouldn't get paid every day like when I babysat for the girls who lived right next door. They wanted to buy me all new school clothes, a winter coat and my school supplies. She told Mom and Dad she would do that for this coming year and for ninth grade and they thought that was more than fair. I thought it was a horrible idea because I would be working all summer without any extra spending money. The weird thing about it was that the woman would still be at the house all day while her husband would be at work.

There were days that she actually left me alone with them, so she could run an errand but her husband or a friend was always with her. She may have thought I was too young, but she soon realized how capable I was. I liked her children and her husband was very nice. We settled into a daily routine and occasionally I would help her with the housework. She often asked me to do that, but Mom had told me to only do it once in a while, that I was only there to watch the children. She had someone come in once a week to do a thorough cleaning.

On one particular day when I was there, she asked me to clean up the kitchen while both girls were down for a nap. When I had finished she came out of her

You're Welcome

bedroom to make a cup of tea and commented on what a wonderful job I had done. I asked her if I could go home for a minute to check on something, but she didn't want me to go. Now, I lived only two houses away from her and would be back lickity-split, but she didn't want me to leave. When I stopped asking to go she came up to me and thanked me for being so understanding. I replied the only way I knew how, "You're welcome."

Now, I did need to go home. I could tell her I was sick, but she wouldn't believe that even if it was true. She would assume that I was saying it so I could go home. I knew the girls would be getting up soon and they would want their snack, so I'd stay for that. When I asked her if she could keep an eye on her own children she finally gave in. I quick ran and got my pillow and backpack and when I came back she thought that I was planning on spending the night. She called Mom and although Mom didn't expect me too, she said that it was okay. Standing now in the living room, I looked around to see where

S. M. Anker

I was going to leave from. I did a slow walk around the inside of the house first and noticed that the window frame in the girl's bedroom was glowing. Their room was on the second floor.

I knew the nausea wouldn't go away until I left but felt that I'd better stay until her husband came home from work. When I thought about that for a few seconds I decided that I could leave. I know I'm spending the night so if I go, the real me will still be expecting to spend the night. I would leave the pillow there and replicate it if I could and we would both have one. I walked over to the window and touched it, but nothing happened. I was going to have to open the window. Still, nothing happened. I looked around to see if something else in the room was pulsating but didn't see anything. Did it want me to climb out the window? I should have been afraid to do that, but I wasn't, so I climbed into the window and jumped out. On the way down I started space running and as I slowed down I touched the ground, but I didn't go

You're Welcome

anywhere in the altered realm. I was standing outside the house. Maybe it knew I wanted my pillow. I thought everything was fine, but I still felt sick. Was I still in the real world?

I immediately went to the window and peeked inside. I was walking into the living room with one of the girls. I had left, but why did I still feel sick? I decided that maybe it wanted me to fulfil my commitment to watch the girls. I only had to wait a short time until her husband came home and walked into the house after him and went right to the bedroom I would be using. I picked up the pillow which replicated and walked downstairs to the back door, which was now pulsating. The rules of this world seemed to be changing. I found it hard to keep up. Mom's rules were always the same. I knew what they were and didn't have to think about them.

When I opened the door and walked out I found myself walking on the deck of a big ship; thank goodness the sick feeling in my stomach was gone. Sometimes I got

S. M. Anker

a bit queasy when I went fishing with my dad if the boat rocked too much. As I walked toward the bow of the ship I saw the name Oriana near the smoke stack. I had heard something on the news about a ship with that name that was going to try to break a record this summer sailing between New Zealand and Australia. I didn't know where we were or what body of water we were in, but if this was that ship, it would be a very cool adventure.

I had come aboard around the supper hour and I was hungry. So far I hadn't gained any extra weight eating in two worlds so I went to hunt down some food.

At first, I followed a couple to see where they were headed and learned, when I heard one of them ask the question, that the ship was ninety-seven feet wide. Then I followed someone else when the couple went to their room and learned that every room on the ship had a radio which was considered a real luxury. They had first class and tourist class on the ship, but I didn't know what that meant.

You're Welcome

As I continued to walk around I would glance in the rooms to see what they were like. I came across a large ball room and saw a swimming pool. I also found out that it took a crew of over nine hundred to run it all. All the walking around had made me even hungrier. I had to find something to eat. I looked at my watch and it was now six thirty and suddenly I saw groups of people walking in the same direction. I followed them.

All the meals served on the ship were sit-down at specific times and now was that time. Since all these people were going to eat, I knew the kitchen would have plenty of food, so I headed out to find it. Following people doesn't always do the trick, but after a few tries, I was in what they called the galley. It was quite hectic, and I saw maybe twenty people there preparing plates. There were about four things to choose from so I grabbed a plate that had a steak on it with mashed potatoes, small carrots and what looked like onions in a red sauce. I took it back to the bow of the ship where I had stashed my backpack and pillow and sat down and ate. The steak was a little too undercooked and I couldn't finish it. I ate the rest of the food but was still hungry, so I went back to the galley. I looked around and found a fresh croissant. There were hundreds of them. I put some ham on it and I had noticed a walk-in refrigerator when I first came in. I went to see if there was anything there to drink and found some chocolate milk that had already been opened. I got a glass and poured some and then walked away. After I had the sandwich, I was satisfied. I did go to the dining room to see what they were having for dessert and took a small dish of ice cream back to the ship's bow.

I put the plate and glass on a tray outside one of the rooms and went looking for a place to sleep later. I followed one of the crew to an area way below all the regular passenger cabin decks into what looked like a special lounge for the crew. It had some tables, couches and chairs. About twenty crew members were relaxing. I thought it was as good a place as any to spend the night if it ever emptied out. After about an hour I overheard a couple of people talking about the crew taking a small dinghy off board if anyone wanted to go. After assisting a smaller ship, they would be put up in a nearby hotel for the night. They had room for about fifteen. A few of them said they wanted to go and were told to get some gear from their rooms. I followed two of them headed in the same direction. They were bunking in this room together with six others. I looked around the area to see if I could find a similar set up for the women but didn't. Then I thought if they left, I'd have a bed to sleep in. It turned out the other six worked the third shift in the kitchen. The room would be completely empty all night. It was only nine when the room became quiet but with the gentle rocking of the ship I fell asleep right away.

I woke in the morning to a noisy bunch coming into the room. The third shift was getting off work which meant breakfast would be served soon and I didn't want to miss it. I found a bathroom and cleaned up and changed my clothes and went into the dining area. I left my pillow back in the bunk room.

I needed to find a table where the people sitting there, had not only just sat down, but also hadn't gotten their food already. I liked what they ordered and when the food came I grabbed one of the plates. No one noticed so I ducked under a table that wasn't being used. I could not believe how clean it was under the table. I mean not even a crumb. I ate a croissant, a soft-boiled egg, a few pieces of ham, and a small bowl of stewed prunes. It all tasted fantastic, but I was curious to see what other people were eating.

As I looked around, it looked like about everyone had the same thing. That meant as long as I got to the dining room I could get whatever was being served for that meal. I had to find out when the meals were going to be served for the rest of the

You're Welcome

day. I figured there had to be a schedule somewhere. Maybe I could also find out where we were.

After breakfast I wandered some more through the decks and generally watched people. I kept going over to people working that had lists or papers to read. If I could see some of them it may give me some answers.

Around ten o'clock all the passengers started moving to the upper deck. They were leaving the ship. Is the ship stopped for good? I ran up to them and from what I heard, they were all going shopping and had to be back on board no later than four in the afternoon. They all had these little books that some official man was looking at.

The man would mark something on his list and ask for the next passenger to come forward. I followed them all out. Some of them got on a bus, so I went with them. We rode for about half an hour and when we got out we were in a downtown setting. I noticed passengers taking off sweaters and light jackets. It must be warm, I thought. I used the time to find out where we were. I ducked into a little store that sold souvenirs. Everything had Australia on it. I walked behind the cash register and looked to see if there was anything showing the city we were in.

It was sitting right there on the counter, a check that the cashier had taken, and on the back was a stamp, For deposit only, One National Bank, Sydney Branch. We were in Sydney. I wrote a book report last year when I was in seventh grade about Australia and decided then that I would go there someday. *'Wow someday had come quickly'.*

I spent the day following people around the city and when I got hungry I followed whoever was going into a restaurant. I wouldn't be able to pay for all the food, let alone the ship, but I'd figure out a way. I would eat on the ship for supper so for now I needed a little something to hold me over. It ended up a sandwich at a nearby deli. Too much

You're Welcome

mustard but I ate the whole thing. I went with this same group of people to the Royal Botanical Gardens.

As a family outing we sometimes went to a botanical garden. It had thousands of flowers and the biggest hills to roll down. During the winter we would take our sleds and go down them on the snow. This park could hold thirty of that park back home. I couldn't believe how big it was. We took a little train around to see everything. They had so many types of flowers and trees I would never remember them all. I looked at my watch and decided I needed to start heading back about the same time the group I was with did. As we got closer and closer, I noticed that the ship was painted completely white. It looked shimmery with the sun behind it now. We all got back in time.

I walked on but they had to go through the same ordeal of having those little books checked. I'd have to see if I could find out what that was all about. Barb would probably know.

S. M. Anker

During supper, I found out that the ship hadn't even left yet for its destination, which was New Zealand. Most of the passengers would be boarding soon and the ship was going to leave port later tonight around eight. The people who were on the ship already came with it from a different location and were traveling on to New Zealand with the same ship. They had taken advantage of a day pass to go sightseeing. The ship was scheduled to be in New Zealand in two days. I decided to stay on board and make the voyage with them. It would be fab.

The people at the table I chose for supper did not speak English. It wasn't Spanish either. I didn't have much luck in Spanish last year so I was going to take it again this fall. Mom told me once that it was okay if I didn't have the aptitude for foreign languages. I didn't start talking until I was three years old and went to speech therapy for a few years. I did like sign language though. I had an aunt that taught at a school for students who were

You're Welcome

deaf. She signed all the time and I talked to her about it more than a couple times. I thought maybe I would like to do that as an interpreter when I got older. My cousins taught me the alphabet when I was nine and still knew it. English was the only language I knew so I had no clue what country my table companions came from. I thought it was interesting that everyone was having the same experience but that when they all went home they would each tell about it in a very different way.

I guess I would say we had an interesting meal. The food was definitely good. I had never had beef wellington but would remember it. I found out that the first class and tourist class had different places to eat. Tomorrow I would try to find out if the tourist class got the same treatment as the first-class passengers. If they did, I'd never spend the extra money to get first class when I was older. All these adventures were sure preparing me for my future life.

S. M. Anker

It was coming up on eight o'clock and the planks for boarding the ship were removed. We were leaving. Everyone was on the top deck looking down at the people who were there to say goodbye. Little by slowly the ship backed out of its slip and into the sea, or ocean, or whatever we were slipping out into. The further out we went the smaller the whole area looked. Before too long we were so far away that all I could see was the sky, the water and another ship not too far away.

The fresh air and the walking I did in town had taken its toll on me. I was very tired now. I was guessing that the crew had gotten back on board before we set sail and would probably be sleeping now before the third shift started. I went looking for the bunk room knowing there should be about six bunks occupied. After about the eighth room, I found it. The crew was asleep, so I grabbed my pillow from behind the desk where I had put it and laid down in one of the empty bunks. I fell asleep quickly.

You're Welcome

The bunk room didn't have a porthole to look out of, so I went up to the main deck to see what the weather was like. It was bright and sunny out. I slept the entire night without waking and hope I didn't miss breakfast.

I found one of the deck bathrooms to clean up in. I ran a comb through my hair and up the stairs I went, taking them two at a time. The dining room was busy with activity. I hadn't missed anything. I looked around for an empty spot and found one where there was a little girl. She looked about three and had the cutest little blond ringlets. She started to talk to me so when they came with the meal I got up and grabbed a plate before it was handed to the passenger and took it to another table with only adults and an empty seat. Today we had French toast, sausages, scrambled eggs and fried apples. People on passenger liners ate well while they were traveling. I spent part of the rest of the morning looking to see if there was a second dining hall for the tourist class passengers and how far it was from this one. When I found it, it was actually in exactly the same place as the first-class dining room except that it was on the floor below it. There was a set of stairs outside both rooms, so I decided when it was lunch time I would first run and see what they were having in tourist and then come upstairs and see what they were having in first class. Then I could decide where I wanted to eat. I would probably be the only passenger to have that option. Now that I had lunch planned, I went about the business of finding out what this trip cost. I know I didn't have that much money but maybe what I had would cover the food.

Lunch came, and the food was different in first class, but I opted for the burgers and fries in tourist class and the people seemed less formal and friendlier. I left some money on the table when I was done to cover my meal. I mixed it in with the tip money I saw one of the passengers leave. After supper, which I took in first class because I thought I would like chicken Marsalis, there was a small band

You're Welcome

playing in one of the lounges. I sat and listened to the music for a while and even got up and danced around since no one could see me. It was fun, and tired me out. I headed for the bunk room and was out like a light before you could say goodnight.

I never heard anything until some crew member came in and told one of the first shift workers to get up because his boss was looking for him. I made a mental note that if I had a job someday, I would have an alarm clock. It sounded like this guy was in trouble for being late.

I got up and walked for a while and finally found the women's bathroom area. I actually found their bunk rooms too, so I went back and grabbed my pillow and stashed it in one of their rooms. I would have to retrace my steps to make sure I knew how to get back for the night. We would be in New Zealand in the morning.

After breakfast, which I took in tourist, I spent most of the day listening to people and walking around the ship. I went into any door that was unlocked. I stood on the bridge and looked out over the water like the Captain. I even jumped in the swimming pool clothes and all. I did make a splash, but no one seemed to notice because there was water spraying all over the place.

I even found a little hospital. There were two beds that looked like the one Bill was in when he had his operation. I guessed that people could get sick on a ship like they could anywhere else. I would have never thought of that though. The people who built the ship did. I had skipped lunch completely because I had way too many corncakes at breakfast. My Dad makes fantastic corncakes and I can eat twenty of them. That's what I did this morning, so I didn't need a lunch. I wasn't very hungry for supper either. It was unusual to feel this way, but I guess I wanted to go home.

I had a good night's sleep and had breakfast already. There were about six pillows in various spots around the bunk rooms that would be around until I went

You're Welcome

back. I didn't need to take one back with me because mine would be there. I had nothing else to do so I found myself first in line to get off the ship when she docked. I wasn't going to wait to get back to Sydney to go home.

Somehow the altered realm knew how badly I wanted to go home. When it was time I walked past the area where they were checking those little books, through a door which was now glowing and pulsating, and right into the front living room where I was babysitting.

I found out later that day, from their father, that the girl's Mom was very ill and couldn't be left alone with the children in case she couldn't take care of them. I worked from eight until six every week day for the rest of the summer.

I didn't see much of Sam, but we talked on the phone. I loved having it in the upstairs hallway. I told her all about my trip on the ship and she told me she wished she could do something neat like that. The rest of the month flew by and before I knew it the local swimming pool was opened. I got there on the weekends whenever I could.

I sometimes got to go to a different park, down by the beach by the big lake, but Mom worried about us when we went there because there was an undertow. She said that if we got caught in it we could be swept out into the middle of the lake without ever realizing it and then it would be too late. The park also had all these pathways and bridges through it and it was fun to explore them and see where we ended up. I carved my initials in one of the bridges so that I could go back when I was older and see if they were still there. That gesture seemed childish compared to what I have experienced this year.

You're Welcome

Chapter Nineteen

They started the new bank next door and it was coming along nicely and would probably be opened in August. Mom found out that there was going to be a drive through window across from her bedroom window and she would hear the cars and the noise from the speaker as early in the morning as seven o'clock. She didn't like it but she thought she could get used to it. There was going to be more traffic closer to the house now because of the number of people it would bring to the shopping area. People seemed to do things in groups. If you go to the bank and there is a grocery store there, then you go to it because it's handy. We will see how the traffic changes once it opens. The Water Fall may certainly get extra day time business.

Babysitting was still my priority in July and it seemed that the girl's father was working longer hours. Sometimes I would be there until eight or nine. I was glad I didn't have to do it on the weekends. The

S. M. Anker

company dad worked for was throwing a huge picnic for all of its employees the second Saturday in July. Helene's birthday would be the next Monday and we were all going to go to the picnic and celebrate her special day. There was nothing Helene liked better than a picnic supper, so it was perfect. I didn't know how many of my friends got to have those kinds of days, the kind you would remember your whole life. I was beginning to be glad that I did.

Sam and I got together the first Saturday which happened to be the fourth and walked to a place where we could watch the parade. It always ended at the park with the pool, so we headed that way. After the parade was over we would stand in line to get a Dixie cup of ice cream and a bag of peanuts. The city always had games and fun things planned for everyone to do but we decided to skip it this year. We ate the ice cream on our way to catch the bus downtown to look at the new summer clothes that were out in the

You're Welcome

big department store windows. We had lunch at Woolworths and went to the public museum. Inside were all sorts of exhibits, from space stuff to when the Indians were hunting buffalo. They even had an enormous dinosaur skeleton. It took us almost four hours to see everything and it was getting late, so we headed home.

We happened to get Barb's bus on the way back. When I said hi to her, Sam looked at me funny. I had told her about Barb but not all of it. I introduced Sam to her before she started the bus up again and we sat in the seats right in front. I had to ask her a question when I got a chance.

One of the next times she stopped I asked if she knew what those book things were that the people were showing on the ship. She told me they were probably passports and that you couldn't leave the country without one. She started to ask why, but anticipating it, I told her that I had to tell her about Australia and gave her a little wink. She understood, and I sat back down next to Sam. "You didn't tell me she knew about, you know what." she whispered.

"Yeah, she does, I had no choice. I got stuck at her house one night and there were three bottles of shampoo and extra towels all over the bathroom. I spent the night there and now I babysit for her." I hadn't told her I helped her out by replicating her.

We got off the bus on the main road a few blocks from the park. We wanted to walk past where they moved the house last month and see if the grass had grown in and what the flowers looked like. The house looked like it had been there for years. We saw the kids playing in the yard so walked away happy it was now home to another family that would probably be there for years. I wondered if our old neighbor had seen it. I'd have to call her. After watching the house for a while, we parted ways. Tonight, after

You're Welcome

supper the family would be going back to the park with the big pool to watch the fireworks.

I was glad when the second week of July was over. I was tired by the time I got home from babysitting the girls. Friday night I was in bed by eight o'clock. I knew we had Dad's company picnic the next day and I wanted to be awake and full of energy.

In the afternoon they would have all kinds of races and games for us to play and contests with prizes. Sometimes we would compete in our own age group and other times there would be things to compete together in with my brothers and sisters. They also had things scheduled for us with our parents. Mom usually watched, but my father liked a challenge as much as I did. Once we did a three-legged race together and won second place.

This year in the morning they had a magician for us. He was only seven years old and the nephew of someone who worked at the company. He lived somewhere in New Jersey and was visiting his uncle for a few weeks. They introduced him as *'Divino the Magnificent.'* I had never seen a magician except on the Ed Sullivan show and I thought he was very, very, good. Richard said that he would probably become famous or something if he kept it up because he was so young. Father thought so too.

For lunch we set up our picnic at one of the tables provided. We had a couple of lawn chairs to sit on, but we left them for Mom and Dad. Mom always brought a blanket or two for us if we wanted to take a nap or rest for a while. The company always grilled the meat and we had to bring what we wanted to go with it. Mom always made potato salad. It was the best I had ever had. She put diced hard-boiled eggs, onion, celery and miracle whip in it and always made it the day before; "So the tastes would blend together," she told me once when I asked. When she put it in the bowl she would sprinkle some paprika

You're Welcome

over the top. Not too much, just enough to make it look pretty.

In addition to the potato salad, there would be a box of chips, buns for the meat, and some celery sticks with peanut butter in the groove. We were also going to have lemon merengue pie for Helene's birthday dessert. Like me, she had several favorites, but Mom had said it would be fine in the cooler. My father would always bring his silver cooler filled with the food and B&B soda.

He would put the soda in the refrigerator the night before and he would buy ice at the gas station that morning. Later when the ice started to melt, the cooler kept everything cold until it was gone. The cooler had this little screw thing on the side and if Dad unscrewed it the water would all pour out. We would fill balloons with the cold water and throw them at each other. It was great on a day like today when it reached eighty degrees. He had that cooler for a very long time, even before he and Mom got married. It's nice to know that my grandfather might have used it at one time. I'm going to remember to have family keepsakes like that to pass on when I'm older.

After lunch the games began. It was my luck that the games for my age group also involved balloons. First was a water balloon toss. I was already dry from the balloons we did earlier, and it was hot enough out that I didn't mind getting wet all over again. In about a half hour I'd be dry.

I am no good at throwing stuff. That's why I never played baseball. My dad did though. He played on a team for the company throwing the picnic. Sometimes they would play at the elementary school near my grandma's house and he would take us with him to watch and cheer him on. He played well and was a great catcher. Not me. As the next balloon came my way, it went right threw my hands and I was not only out, I was drenched. When that game ended, and the prizes were awarded we moved right

You're Welcome

into the next one. This time we worked in teams of two.

We all had to stand in a line and put ourselves tallest to shortest. I was pretty tall, already taller than Amelia, so I was further forward in the line than she was. It didn't matter though because what they were doing was getting us a partner that had the same chin height.

When the adults were through pairing us off, one of us had to put a water balloon under our chin and then pass it to the other. When we passed it successfully the person without the balloon had to take a small step forward. We had a finish line that we had to take the balloon across but if I moved to far away it was harder for my partner to pass the balloon. It was a very slow process. If I dropped the balloon and it did not explode, I could go back to the beginning and start over. If it exploded, we were both out.

It was hard but about fifteen minutes into the challenge we noticed that there were only three teams left. Ours was one of them. We decided that we would pass quicker if we were pretty close and moved only a little at a time, so we kept doing that. We moved about two inches at a time. We had to be careful not to rush.

Then the team closest to us dropped their balloon but it didn't explode. They didn't want to forfeit third place, so they started over. The next team was too far away because they too had to start over earlier. We took our time and another five minutes we were across the finish line and the girl grabbed the balloon and pulled me closer to her and threw the balloon up in the air and it came down, splash, and got us all wet.

"We did it." she screamed towards her mother. She and I each got an early release of a record by the Herman's Hermits, the newest band to come out of England. The record was called, "I'm into Something Good." I had never heard of them so wasn't sure if I would like it, but we also got a large bag of salted peanuts in the shell, and a voucher for ten dollars from the Dairy Dutch.

You're Welcome

The whole family played games most of the afternoon. I watched as my younger sisters and brother played their games and got to help Ellen in one that she was doing involving a jump rope. She got excited because we took second place and she got a doll that had its own buggy. At the end of the games we generally ran around and played.

Then a couple of dozen adults passed out individual presents and bags of treats to all of the children three and under. During this time, a different group of adults roped off an area about the size of a block. It was huge. In the roped off area the adults took buckets filled with all kinds of stuff and sprinkled it everywhere.

When they were all done every child from four to sixteen got a bag and then all the children ages four, five and six had to line up along one side. When the rope dropped, they had to make their way across the field to the other side where some parents were calling to them. They each had a bag and if they found something on the grass they could pick it up and put it in their bag. They had twenty minutes to do this.

Then the adults went back out and added stuff to the field. When they were done the seven and eight-year-olds got to go but they only had fifteen minutes to do this. And again, the adults went out and added stuff.

The nine and ten-year-olds had ten minutes to do it. I was in the eleven and twelve-year-old group and after the adults added stuff again, we had seven minutes on the field. Then they split the field in half and added stuff and the five through ten-year-olds got to go on one side until they couldn't find anything anymore. Our side was opened to anyone eleven through sixteen. We also got to look until we couldn't find anything. We all had bags that were stuffed. I got tons of gum, some pennies, a few nickels; I even had a dollar bill. I picked up some cards, a ball and jacks, six little boxes of raisins, this paddle ball game, a rain umbrella, suntan lotion, and even more candy. Mom almost had a

You're Welcome

heart attack when all nine of us showed up with our bags. We took in quite the haul.

This event was the final planned activity for the day and about an hour afterwards people started packing up to go home. It took us a while but when all of us were in the car in our special places, Dad asked "Anyone for Dairy O?" It had been a wonderful day and I had so much fun with the family.

Mom had all of us in bed by nine o'clock, even Richard and Amelia, although Amelia stayed awake for a long while because when I got up to use the bathroom around eleven she was still drawing. Not me, I went back to bed and was asleep right away.

In the morning after church we got hot ham and rolls for breakfast. After I read the cartoons in the Sunday paper, I picked up the travel section. I never looked in it before but the trip on the ship was still fresh and I wanted to see if I could find out what something like that cost. I never found out when I was there. I was surprised at how many things they offered from the travel agencies. Bus tours to Las Vegas, four-day holidays to the Bahamas, they even had packages listed for places like the Kentucky Derby and Mardi Gras.

I knew I couldn't plan a trip and go because although my adventures usually took place sometime at the end of the month, I was never sure exactly when it would happen. The best I could do was make some plans that I could duplicate no matter what day of the week I left. If I wanted to go to Florida, for instance, if there was a plane that left every day at the same time I could catch it no matter what day I entered the altered realm.

Looking now, I did see that the standard tourist rate for a passenger liner was about two hundred and fifty dollars. First class could cost as much as four hundred dollars or more. Most of the ads, however, said that passengers, thirteen and under accompanied by an adult were free. I felt better knowing I would be free. I had only given out a few tips when I was on the ship. I called a few of the travel

You're Welcome

agencies during the week, when the kids I was watching were sleeping, to find out more about the cruises. I pretended I was a grown up and they answered every question I had. I found out that the meals I got on the ship were included in the fare and the only extra expense to me was tipping and if you went off the ship into one of the towns. When you did that it was called an excursion. I also checked on the thirteen and under condition and she said that many of the ships still had it but that some of them were changing the age to twelve and under.

I remembered to thank her for her help and she said, "You're welcome." She giggled. Then she said, "I don't know why I laughed at you, please forgive me if I sounded rude." I had to smile to myself and told her not to worry about it and said, "Goodbye and have a great day."

Now wait a minute. I had thought all this time that Richard, Arthur and Amelia giggling meant that they had been on adventures when they were twelve. Sam said she didn't. Had the lady I was talking to have her own adventures? Was it all me? If I was provoking the response in them, I had to find out why.

I had a good idea by the end of the week what I would do for Sam's surprise. I had most of it written down, so I could keep it all straight. I also planned that we would do it next month before we started going to eighth grade. It would be perfect.

About ten days passed before I heard myself saying "You're welcome." to my little sister Ellen after she thanked me for a piggy back ride around the backyard. I took her with me into the house and looked around. I didn't see anything. I hoped it would happen fast because for some reason I felt sicker than usual. Mom asked me to put Ellen down for a nap as long as we were done playing and there it was. The double bed she slept in was pulsating all over the place. I wondered if she would feel it. I tucked her in and gave her one of her favorite baby dolls, but she wanted her new one that she had gotten at the picnic. I put her Little Ellie doll back on her shelf and turned around to give her the new one, but she was fast asleep already. I ran downstairs to get my backpack and Mom yelled "Stop running on those stairs!"

"Sorry," I said, grabbed the bag, and walked back up to Ellen's room. I would have to see if she remembers if the bed rocked her to sleep. I lay down next to her and when the nausea disappeared, I was in my own bed. I went to sleep. I don't know how long I was asleep, but Ellen came into my room and asked me to make it stop. "Make what stop?"

"The bed." she said, "It won't stop bouncing me around." I went into her room and sure enough the bed was pulsating. I crawled into bed with her and we both fell asleep. I heard Mom call upstairs that supper was on the table, so I woke her up, we washed up, and went down to eat. She told me that she didn't like the bouncy bed and I told her it wouldn't happen again. That was that, she had felt it. Maybe it had something to do with how old she was. I remembered that the little puppy could tell I was there in the altered realm even though it was in the real world. I also thought the little child on the carriage ride could see me. Ellen would be four in a few months.

I went to the altered realm and had already come back in less than a couple of hours. Maybe what I was doing prior to leaving had something to do with what type of adventure I would have. I was enjoying my time with Ellen and perhaps the altered realm knew that. I was guessing but if that was my adventure for the month, it was done. It was probably a good thing because I had all sorts of things planned for the next time if it happened again. How was I supposed to know when it was going to end? I hoped that wasn't the end of it.

Chapter Twenty

As August got started I had been given permission to take the girls I was watching up to the park to go under the sprinklers they had installed. We could play there for hours and they wouldn't get bored. Sometimes I would pack a lunch and lay a blanket under the elephant tree and eat there. The girls would fall asleep and I would listen to my transistor radio. When they would wake up we'd go play in the sprinklers again. It was a good way to keep them occupied and gave their Mom some much needed rest.

I called Sam to tell her that I had a late birthday present for her that I had been working on but that she might not get it until later in the month. Of course, she wanted me to tell her what it was, but I told her she would have to wait.

"Then why did you say anything at all, you know I can't wait." She said angrily.

"So, you would have time to anticipate it." I had heard Mom say that once.

"Well, okay then, I'll just anticipate." She laughed so I knew she wasn't mad.

Nearer to the end of August we celebrated Richard's sixteenth birthday. He liked Mom's meatloaf so that was his birthday supper. It was a good celebration, but he didn't hang around for his pinch to grow and inch. "I'm not going to grow any bigger than I am, so I don't need it anymore." He was dead serious. Not me, I'd take them until I was taller than everyone in the family.

I found out that the woman I was babysitting for was feeling much stronger and even came with us once to the park. I wasn't sure what was wrong, but all her hair fell out earlier and she was wearing the most beautiful scarves wrapped like a turban on her head. I didn't ask Mom, although she probably would have told me the truth. I guess I didn't want to know. It was good to see her feeling better and the girls were happy when she was able to start spending more time with them.

You're Welcome

I couldn't decide if I should clue Sam in on what was going to happen or simply do it. I'd have to see. It happened with my father this time. I was watching television with him in the living room about ten in the morning and he asked me to get him a River Green soda. I was never allowed a B&B soda that early in the morning. I did what he asked and he said, "Thank you." and before I knew it I had that nauseating feeling in my stomach, the words "You're welcome." barely out of my mouth.

I ran and got my stuff, a bit more than usual because I had put a few extra items in. One of the last times I had been at Sam's to sleep over I took some of her things. A pair of pants, some underwear, socks, a shirt, a pair of her pajamas, one of her combs, and some of her hair barrettes. I had enough of the other stuff that we could share. I did throw an extra new toothbrush in the bag though.

Then I called Barb and said, "Purple Socks." to her and hung up. I looked around to see what was pulsating or glowing but didn't find anything. I looked everywhere. I was standing on the bed looking out the window and saw it on the ground. The sidewalk was doing its thing again. I walked down the stairs, so Mom wouldn't yell and then out the back door. It wouldn't have mattered because Mom saw me; she was watering the flowers in her special garden and asked, "Where you headed?"

"Over to Marley's remember?" I still called her that once in a while. Mom would expect it when the real 'me' said it when I was in the altered realm.
"Remember what?" she said.
"I'm staying overnight a few nights because I don't have to watch the girls for the next week." "He's taking them with him when they go back to see the doctor and then he's off work the rest of the week cause he's interviewing for those jobs I told you about."
"Oh yeah, I forgot, have fun."
"Thanks Mom." I know Mom missed me, but she still had eight other kids to

keep her busy. I gave her a kiss and was on my way.

I ran down the street stepping on each of the pulsating slabs so I didn't miss any of them. As I was getting ready to turn the block towards Sam's house I had to stop in my tracks. The slabs to either side of me were no longer pulsating. I looked around and to the side of me in a person's yard was a little house. It was the size that my sister Ellen would be able to play in. The door on the little house was glowing and I walked over to it. There was a little girl in the house pretending that she was cooking supper on a little stove. Then the handle on the door started to pulsate so I grabbed it.

When the sick feeling left I was standing back on the sidewalk and kept walking to Sam's house. I also saw myself walking to Sam's house. I waited until I rang the doorbell and walked into the house with myself. Sam's Mom told me that she was waiting for me upstairs and to tell her when I got there that we were all going out for pizza for lunch. I watched and listened to everything waiting for a good time to surprise her. I decided to go with them for pizza since I hadn't had anything to eat for a while. When we got back we had the room to ourselves.

We were having a conversation and Sam stood up to get something off the shelf above the bed. If I was going to pick her up and replicate her it had to be now. I gathered up all my strength and grabbed her around the legs and lifted her as high as I possibly could. Like Barb, she fell, only backwards onto me. I broke her fall but we both landed on the floor. She was looking straight at me and said, "What the heck did you do that for?" and I told her that I had to. I said, "Turn around." She was staring at the two of us sitting on the bed looking at the book she had taken off the shelf. Then she looked at me and then she looked back at us on the bed. It took a few minutes, but it finally sunk in and I yelled "Surprise!"

I thought she was going to freak out! She was screaming hysterically and ran down stairs and then back up and looked again at us sitting on the bed "They are still there." she said.

"Of course, they are." "Now sit down a minute and let me explain." I told her what I had done for Barb when Bill was in the hospital and how it all worked out. I explained that I couldn't tell her that part of the story because at the time I had too many questions. I said, "I didn't feel right springing it on you before I figured it out." I told her she would retain all the memories and that we were going to have a wicked cool time.

She looked me square in the eye and said, "What are we going to do first?" I laughed and told her that I had my backpack packed and that I had some of her things too. I explained all about the replicating process and how things, including her, would disappear when I went back to the real world. I had almost twenty dollars and asked her if she had any money. She checked the pockets of the pants she was wearing and she found twelve dollars. I told her we would need to try to pay for things when we could. I said "First stop is State Fair Park. It's still early enough."

Usually we would take the bus, but it was a beautiful day out and I couldn't wait to show Sam how to run in space. I hadn't even shared that tidbit with Barb. After I explained it and showed her how it was done, we did a few trial runs. First; up to the end of the block and back, then to my house and back. Once she thought she had the hang of it we headed down the streets in the same way we would go on the bus. It was the only way we knew how to get there.

It took about twenty minutes because we weren't space running very fast. Once we got there we stood in line like everyone else and moved up when we were supposed to. We didn't have to do that, it seemed like the right thing to do. As we went in we dropped our money into the box the ticket seller was using but no one even noticed. The first thing we did was go on almost all the rides.

You're Welcome

We went through the House of Mirrors at least five times and the Fun House even more than that. It had this huge barrel like thing that spun around and around. We had to start on one side and walk through it as it was turning, and we would fall down laughing so hard we couldn't get back up. It was so much fun that we kept trying until we got all the way through on one try.

There were all kinds of shows set up in tents and outdoor areas all over the park. We got to see all of the 'Kids of the Heartland' show. It featured children seven to sixteen from all over the United States who tried out and were selected. The show went to as many state fairs as they could get to during the summer. It was our luck they were here.

We started to get hungry and there were only two things we both wanted; corn on the cob and cream puffs. Sam made the mistake of setting her corn down and picking it up so there were two of them. She was full from the first one though and left it because I told her it would be there no matter how many times she picked it up. We replicated so many things during the day. When we left the animal barn we could still hear someone asking, "Where did all these chickens come from?"

As the day went on she got the hang of it. I could tell it was starting to get cooler out. Not because we were cold, but I noticed people pulling out sweaters from bags or purses. Sam asked me if I brought one for her and I told her she wouldn't need it. "But if I do, did you bring one?" I asked how she had felt all day and she answered that she was very comfy. "Not sweaty or hot like everyone else?"

"Not at all." "What a hoot, I get it. I can't feel the temperature, can I?"

"Nope isn't it wonderful!"

As the night progressed we decided to stay for the grandstand show. Peter, Paul and Mary were playing, and the show was free when we bought our tickets to get in. We had to be careful where we sat. We chose the good seats and if someone came and looked like they were going to sit on us, we would move. No one did so we had front and center seats for the entire show.

Afterwards we wandered over to the hill where we could watch the evening fireworks. They always had the coolest stuff shooting off from the ground and all kinds of special displays. Usually we couldn't get close enough to see any of it. We did this time. The fireworks lasted almost forty-five minutes.

Sam wanted to know what we were going to do for the night. I told her we were going to go to Barb's. She would leave the door open if it was after she went to bed and we would use the spare room. We had to be sure if she wasn't up to lock the door when we got in. In the morning she would bring us breakfast.

It was all arranged. So off we went space running again on the streets the bus ran because, frankly, I didn't know how to get anywhere otherwise. I knew there was probably a shorter way, but this made it easy. Sam agreed, and we were there in about eight minutes. The lights were all off in the house, but true to her word, Barb had left the front door open and we locked up. Sam and I used the downstairs bathroom to get ready for bed and although we didn't need to, walked very quietly up the stairs.

We were getting into the big double bed when suddenly we heard the faintest of whispers "I heard you come in, I was up to change Jean Rae, have a good rest and I'll talk to you in the morning." Then she was gone. I was wondering how she heard us come in since she wasn't in the altered realm with us. Maybe it was because she had come into it once before. I'd have to talk to her about it. Sam said to me "This was some total stranger that you decided to help and now she is helping us?"

"Neat, isn't it?" "Mom always says 'people are more important than things' if you're nice to people, people will be nice to you." I started to tell Sam that I was surprised that Barb heard us and that she shouldn't have been able to. Before I

You're Welcome

finished the sentence, Sam was asleep. I followed right behind her.

In the morning, I heard a knock at the door and saw Barb walking in with a huge tray of food. She had made bacon and cheese omelets. There were two glasses of milk, buttered rye toast and some black raspberry jam. She set it down on the dresser and left. I assumed she was also having breakfast with Bill and Jean Rae downstairs.

After Bill went to work, Barb asked if I could keep an eye on Jean Rae for about an hour while she did some grocery shopping. Sam reached out to Jean Rae when she reached out to her. Sam was astonished and asked if the baby could see us. I told her that it appeared that babies and young animals can. Maybe it's because they can't talk and tell. I hadn't figured that out. I was sure though, that Jean Rae could. I had missed her. I did feel like her big sister. I was trying to figure out why there were not two of her. That was strange. I let Sam take care of her, so I wouldn't replicate her.

S. M. Anker

When Barb got back she had more than groceries with her. She had stopped by her bank and handed us each two hundred dollars. She brought out the writing tablet and I asked her what that was for. She said it was a 'thank you' for all the help I gave her when Bill was in the hospital. I wrote that she had already thanked me enough.

The next thing she said out loud blew our minds. It seems that when she was replicated, one of the errands she ran was slipping up north to a casino. They usually went there together once a month and he couldn't go with her this time. She had two hundred dollars with her and she played the slot machines. She said she was trying to win a little to help cover the cost of Bill's hospital stay.

When she went to cash in her money, she slipped the teller her buckets of coins. The teller could see the buckets but not where they came from and assumed it was for the next person in line. The teller set down more than fourteen hundred dollars. She said she was very happy with

You're Welcome

that, but when he set it down on the counter he pushed it through the window opening and I had to pick it up. "I picked it up, about twenty times." she told us. "I went nuts!"

The teller that helped me left after my transaction and I couldn't get anyone else's attention. The guy in line went to a different teller and I had to stop at some point and I walked away leaving the fourteen hundred dollars on the counter. I waited on the side to see if someone would take it, but when the guy came back it was still there. I don't know if he ended up keeping it or not. I, on the other hand, walked away with more than twenty-five thousand dollars. I knew I should have stopped after the first few times it was still there, but I got carried away and thought it would stop. I tried to gamble it back to them but kept winning. I left some of it in a bunch of machines for the next person that sat down. I finally had to get back to my to-do list and took what was left home with me. I paid off all of Bill's medical bills that the insurance didn't cover and I set up a college fund for Jean Rae. I thought I would keep some here for you for when you needed it. If I run into a pinch and need it for food or something, I'll use it for us. "I didn't know what else to do." she said.

Mom would have said that gambling was not a good thing to start. I still may try it when I get older to see what all the talk is about. I told her that I was surprised the money didn't disappear when I went back into the real world and that she had to do something good with what she had left and that I didn't want anymore. She said she thought that it would have disappeared too. "When it didn't I wrote in my notebook, wait I'll go get it." When she came back she read this out of it. "I don't know what I'm going to do with all this money. I know that when Sas leaves the altered realm, the altered me disappears and I am myself. The money I got at the Casino isn't something Sas replicated. I replicated it and it didn't disappear. Sas may need to know that."

You're Welcome

I didn't know exactly what that would mean in the long run but thanked her for the observation and remembering to write it down for me. The next thing I asked Barb was how many Jean Rae's she saw, and she answered "One." So maybe the owner of those chickens wouldn't have to buy a larger coop after all.

We visited with Barb and Jean Rae for about another hour, but I was killing time until we took the next step on our adventure. When it was about ten thirty we said our goodbyes, I gave Jean Rae a kiss on the cheek and we were off. From Barb's house I knew exactly which direction to space run and we were at the airport in about fifteen minutes.

Sam and I had often gone to the airport with my parents to watch the airplanes take off and land, but neither of us had ever flown anywhere to see what that was like. I told her we were going to look inside one of the airplanes before it took off and she thought that was really neat.

There were large lists on the walls that had boarding times for each airline. The

S. M. Anker

airport had three different airlines. I was looking for North Central and found it in the third row. Flight two sixty-one was going to depart at gate two at eleven thirty and was on time. That is all I needed to know. I told Sam that we had to wait until everyone else was seated. Then we could walk on and look around or go up front where first class was. Maybe we would even see the captain sitting in the cockpit.

"May I have your attention, please, will all those passengers in first class, or those with small children or in need of extra assistance, please have your boarding passes ready, we will be boarding in a few minutes." There were several men in business suits that stood up, one woman with two small children in a stroller, and one man sitting in a wheelchair who all got in line. When they were boarded another announcement came on for different rows in the plane.

We waited until the last section was called and lingered behind the last couple we saw boarding. Once we were inside and everyone else was seated, we looked around and were amazed at how big it looked inside. I pulled Sam toward the front of the plane because if I had done my homework right there would be four or five empty seats in the first-class section and we were going to use two of them. Sam followed me, and I was right, there were six of the twelve seats empty. I said to her to pick the two seats she wanted to try out and she went immediately for the ones by the biggest window. We sat down, her by the window and me next to the aisle.

I made it seem like we were pretending to be real passengers almost up to the point when the announcement from the captain started. "Welcome to North Central Airlines, flying this wonderful summer morning to the City of New York. Flying time today will take under two hours depending on the gale winds. Please have a pleasant trip." Sam looked at me and said, "we better get off or we are going to be stuck going to New York!" I looked at her for a few minutes then smiled and yelled "Surprise!"

The time went faster than I thought it would and looking down at the small houses, roads and cars was wonderful. Sam thought for a minute that she might get sick, but the feeling went away and she was actually enjoying the flight. Since we could not be seen, the stewardesses were not serving us lunch. When it was safe, we got up and went to the galley, which is also what a plane calls its kitchen, and picked a plate of food and hoped for the best. We both got a roast beef sandwich with a pickle on the side, a bag of chips and I found us two sodas. It was enough to hold us until supper.

The landing was a little scary for both of us, but we made it safe and sound. As we were walking out of the plane I saw the captain handing out little wings to two small children. One said, "Do you want one too?"

I said "Yes, please," and the young boy said, "Two please for my friends?"

The captain said "Why sure, young man. Here you go, for your imaginary friends." The boy got them and handed them to us. There wasn't any left in his hand when he did that. I told Sam that we had to make a note of that because that was different altogether. We didn't pick up the wings they were handed to us. If something is handed to us it won't replicate. "Did you get all that down?" Sam said she did. Not sure what good it will do us in the future unless people are giving free stuff away. It was probably a good thing to know.

I told Sam that we were staying at any hotel we saw people walking into. We followed a couple of women that looked like they knew where they were headed. They did indeed, for about nine blocks later we were walking into the Old Broadway Hotel. They were staying in a room on the third floor and while they were getting their key, I was standing behind the clerk looking at the register. Two rooms on the eight floor were empty during the time we would be there, so I grabbed the keys to one of them off the rack behind me.

S. M. Anker

Sam and I rode the elevator up and when we got off we had to look around for a bit. I didn't see the room number of the key anywhere on the floor we got off on. We took the elevator back down to the main floor and as we were getting out I saw it, a button for Eight PH. I pushed that button. Nothing happened. Then I saw another little sign next to it that said, must insert key to execute. I put the key in the lock and turned it then pushed the button and away we went. When the door opened this time, we were not in a hallway. We were in the room, or penthouse as it turned out. It was like everything we ever saw in the glamour magazines. "Are we going to stay here?" Sam asked.

I answered "For the next two days and then we head home. I hope that is long enough." Sam asked, "Long enough for what?" I told her that she would see in the morning but that now we needed to get supper and go to bed so we could get up early. I called the clerk downstairs and asked them to give Penthouse eight a seven o'clock wake-up call. The clerk said, "Why of course Madame' but I didn't think you were coming in for another few days."

"My plans had to change, and I want to get out early tomorrow morning." The clerk said, "Very good Madame' seven tomorrow then." I was surprised he didn't know that my voice was different since he acted like he knew who was calling.

The phone call in the morning startled me for a second as I climbed out of the luxurious bed I chose to sleep in. It was so big; more than four of me could have slept comfortable.

The call also woke Sam. So the day began. We ordered room service and told them to set it up in the lounge area. We hid in one of the rooms until we heard the waiter leave and then feasted on two gourmet breakfasts. We had freshly squeezed orange juice, something called eggs benedict with Hollandaise sauce, ham and a toasted cinnamon muffin. It was all very yummy and a great start to the day. We left some money on the cart to cover the food and placed it in the elevator and sent it down.

After getting dressed we were ready to leave and I hadn't told Sam yet where we were going. We walked down to the front of the hotel and when a limousine showed up for someone, we climbed in. The driver asked where the gentleman wanted to go. He gave some address close to where we needed to be in Queens. When we got there and got out, Sam saw what I did.

Right across the street in front of us was a very large Unisphere. A twelve-story high, spherical stainless-steel copy of the Earth that had been commissioned for the World's Fair. In front of the Unisphere were colorful flags from all the different countries involved in the Fair.

Sam didn't get what it meant. "This is my surprise?" she asked.

Once I explained to her where we were and told her that we would be there for the next two days, she got excited.

You're Welcome

We stood in line for a long time to pay our one-dollar admission and proceeded to see everything we could from the Unisphere to all the exhibits. We enjoyed the US Space Park and the 'world's largest cheese' exhibit from Wisconsin.

We also saw an exhibit that featured the use of something called a computer main frame which was very large and noisy. It was similar to my Think-a-Tron in that it used special cards that had holes punched in them. The demonstrators told us that within thirty years computers would be a common thing found in businesses and homes. I found that hard to believe unless they were going to make them much smaller. We also saw the Vatican Pavilion where they had a statue on display done by Michelangelo. In addition, we found a place serving waffles with strawberries and whipping cream. The only thing missing were the rides. For some reason they didn't have a midway anywhere we could find.

We had a great first day and even better second day as we hung around the Seven-

S. M. Anker

Up tent most of the day. They had all types of sandwiches there to try from different countries and international music was playing most of the time. Seven Up had its own band, but occasionally when they took a break, some person or group of persons would be there with instruments of their own to fill in with the music of their culture. It was wonderful.

As it started getting late that second day, we needed to head to the hotel and get our things and get to the airport. Sam shared with me that she didn't want to go home, and I laughed. I was glad she was having fun. We got a ride from the same limousine driver we had earlier. He was taking a group to the airport in one of the hotel transport buses. I knew we were flying at seven thirty on a North Central flight, so we had some time to watch people in the airport. In the airport there were many people saying goodbye and as many were having happy reunions. I found myself missing my family more than other trips into the altered realm. I was glad Sam was here with me. I

You're Welcome

wondered what she would say about her final surprise.

When the announcement from the captain came on, it was the first time Sam learned we were headed for Los Angeles, California. She knew right away where we were going. We had talked about it at least a couple of dozen times in the last two years.

We got to Disneyland the next morning and took the monorail around the park first so that we could, as my father would put it 'get the lay of the land.' Neither of us was any good reading the maps so we wandered around until we saw something we wanted to do. We took a ride on the double decker bus and could get on and off whenever it stopped.

We visited Main Street USA, and Adventure Land during the morning. We must have ridden the Big Thunder Mountain Railroad a dozen times when we got to Frontierland before lunch. The slow steady speed of the Mark Twain Riverboat was perfect after we ate, and they were serving something called nonalcoholic Mint Juleps and they were delicious.

Tomorrowland wasn't opened because it was undergoing renovations and would not reopen for a few years so we didn't get to see it but Fantasyland was fun. We got to pretend we were flying with Peter Pan and we rode King Arthur's Carrousel so much we got dizzy. As the day ended we had to return to reality and go home. One thing for sure, we got to create memories that both of us would have.

We took a plane home at about ten that evening and landed around one thirty in the morning. I didn't know if I could get back to the real world, so I checked to see if the little house on the way to Sam's was glowing. Everything looked dark and it was too late to get into Sam's house, so we cuddled up inside the little girl's playhouse and fell asleep. The light in the morning woke us up and we got to Sam's house as her father was leaving for work, so we went in right to the basement.

We talked about everything we had done and Sam said that it was the best surprise she ever had. We both fell back to sleep on the stage.

Later in the afternoon I had to go see if it was time to go back so I walked down the block to the little girl's playhouse again. It was glowing this time, so I grabbed the doorknob which was pulsating and a moment later I was back at Sam's up in her room. She looked at me and said, "Purple socks."

I told her I needed to head home and asked her if she was okay. She said she felt good and remembered all the stuff we did. She still had a few dollars in her pocket though that didn't disappear. If she carried it into the altered realm or replicated it there, it didn't disappear. I'm guessing it was because Barb gave it to her. "Put it in the collection basket at church Sunday, that's what I'm going to do." She thanked me again for her surprise and said she hoped we could do it again. I told her I didn't know how many more of these adventures I would have but at least she got to go on one. I headed home. The rest of August was spent babysitting for the girls. Their Mom was so much better, and I would be able to stop once school started. I found myself spending more time at home with my family when I wasn't babysitting. That urge to get away from them wasn't as strong as it had been.

You're Welcome

Chapter Twenty-One

After Labor Day many of the stores were having sales and when I went to watch the girls on Tuesday their Mom said that if I wanted I could go shopping now for new school clothes and a winter coat. She said that I could get anything that my parents approved and there was no limit to what I could buy. I went shopping with my dad and got several new skirts and a few sweaters, four blouses and three pair of stretch pants and five pair of tights. I also bought three new dresses and a white pin stripped shirt with navy blue stripes. I had seen one in the glamour magazine and it said that everyone should have one. It made my eyes dizzy looking at it for too long. I got two pair of shoes, some socks and underwear, a pair of tennis shoes, a pair of boots and new mittens. Dad let me get a new pair of jeans too, but we weren't sure she would pay for those because I'm not allowed to wear them in school.

Then I got to pick out my winter coat. There were so many styles to choose from.

S. M. Anker

I picked out a very heavy, warm, green corduroy coat with large gold buttons. It had two slanted side pockets and the prettiest fur collar. I almost couldn't wait for it to get cold out so I could wear it. Dad paid for everything and I took the receipt to the women and she gave me cash to take back to my dad. She even paid for the jeans. She gave me an extra one hundred dollars and told me to tell him it was for my school supplies and that if I needed anymore to have me come by and get it and that if it was too much to spend it on the other children's supplies. I saw my dad's eyes tear up. I was glad that I had worked so hard all summer to help. Dad said it helped me learn about work ethic and that now I would have that my whole life.

Our classes started on Friday that same week I went shopping. The first week of classes felt a bit strange. It always felt like that after the summer was over. I am not a morning person and would rather sleep until noon every day and have classes in the evenings. Even though I had gotten

You're Welcome

up early to babysit the girls I didn't have to be there until eight in the morning. It was going to take me a while to get into the routine and having to get up even earlier to get to the bus stop by seven-thirty didn't help. Mom said I should have started a couple of weeks earlier so that I would be ready for it by the time classes started, but I didn't listen to her. Moms seem to know more than we do for a reason.

Earlier this year they started work on the new High School. I still had a year left at the school behind the tracks so next fall would be the first year that the old high school would become the junior high. That meant that elementary schools would only go to sixth grade and the junior high would have seventh, eighth, and ninth grades and the high school would have tenth, eleventh and twelfth.

I would be in the last eighth grade class in the school behind the tracks and the very first ninth grade class in the junior high. And I would only be there one year and then I'd go to the high school.

Richard would be in the first graduating class from the new high school.

There would be many firsts in the next few years. It started with the new bank next to us opening the following Monday.

Sam and I tried to meet up for homework after school at least twice a week, but our teachers were teaching different things in the same subjects so it wasn't much help. Still I was happy to do homework with her. She still got to go home for lunch, but I had to stay at school and eat in the cafeteria. Most days I took a lunch unless I knew they were having something good. Some days, if I had money, I would have both. Occasionally I would walk home from school if I stayed after for something. The colder out that it got, the more I came to love my new coat.

I found myself going over to see the girls on the weekends because I missed them. They missed seeing me too. Their Mom was completely well and got out quite a bit. She was a social butterfly in her circle of friends and they were happy to have her back.

You're Welcome

I got so busy, I only talked to Barb once since we had gotten back from Los Angeles and that was to thank her for all her help. She wanted to know if I could watch Jean Rae the following weekend. I checked with Mom before calling her back to tell her I could.

She said she was working Saturday until four o'clock and my route was the last on her run that day. If I met her at the bus stop around four ten, I could ride with her back to the bus graveyard and then home with her.

After school Friday, Sam and I went to the first football game of the season. We lost to another nearby high school, but the game was still good. We went to the Dairy Dutch afterwards for a haystack and a coke. I got home around nine thirty and Mom asked me to lock up the back door and turn the light off. "Okay, I got it."

She said "Thanks." and I couldn't stop myself. I said, "You're welcome."

It's not that I didn't want to go on another adventure; I was looking forward to babysitting for Jean Rae tomorrow. I had arranged with Barb to watch Ellen for the evening with Jean Rae. Anyway, I grabbed my backpack and looked around.

I was getting better at looking because sometimes the place wasn't very obvious. This time I saw the door on the cubby in the hallway pulsating. The cubby was the area above the stairs going to the basement.

When Mom made Christmas cookies beforehand she stored them in containers in the cubby because it isn't heated and they stayed fresh. She starts so far in advance of Christmas that when she locks it up we are supposed to believe that she is keeping us from getting to the cookies. They really hid the Christmas presents in there. Tonight, I didn't know what I would find inside.

As I put my hand on the handle I half expected to be totally whisked away immediately, but I had to open the door, then I had to go inside, then I closed the door and sat there. I knew I wasn't gone yet because my stomach still felt sick, so I looked around. Something in that cubby had to be pulsating. I even looked for the glow.

I turned my head and there, I saw something. When I turned my head the other way it was gone. So naturally, I moved my head around some more and I saw it again. What did I see? Then I got it! It was my glasses. I took them off and the frame was glowing. I held it in my hand and nothing happened. I put them on my face again, and nothing happened. I couldn't figure out what I needed to do so I jumped out of the cubby and went upstairs.

As I glanced in the mirror, I caught a glimpse of a glow on the bow of the frame, so I took them off again and held the bow in both hands. Nothing happened. I folded them and set them down on the dresser. That was it. Next thing I knew, I was inside the cubby and needed to climb back out.

I had left my backpack and pillow in the cubby when I went upstairs so when I went to the altered realm I didn't have it. I could see it there in the cubby with me, so knowing everything in it would replicate anyway, I left it behind. I did grab my pillow though. I opened the cubby door to jump out into the back hallway and when I jumped, I landed beneath the elephant tree.

I wondered what I was doing there, but there wasn't anything to guide me anywhere, so I started walking, trying to decide what I wanted to do. Then it came to me. I could take a train ride up north to see Nanny. I hadn't seen her in a while. I could have run through space to get there, but I liked being on a train and this time I would be in a passenger car not a freight car.

It was a good thing that I had taken all my money with me to the game in case I needed it for something to eat. I left some on the train when I got off at my stop. Nanny was at the tavern she owned, and I went inside. It was good to see her even if she couldn't see me. I had helped her wash glasses when I was there earlier this summer. There was this sink that was divided into two. In one side was a brush

You're Welcome

on a metal rod. The other side had clear water. I would have to take a glass and turn it upside down over the drain to empty any beer that was inside. Then I would put it on the brush and turn the glass around and around until it was all sudsy. Next, I rinsed the glass in the clear water and set the glass upside down on the drain board.

I enjoyed being at the tavern. The smell was unique and even when I was home if I thought about it hard enough I could still smell it. Nanny had lived in the back of the tavern for years, but she moved to this big white house up on the hill with my uncle. I walked over there for a bit to see if my cousins were around, but they must have been away for the night. I walked around the house across the street where friends of ours lived but I didn't see them at all, so I walked back to the tavern. It was never very busy, but there was always someone there. I was going to go there and drink my first beer when I was old enough. For the heck of it, I was watching one guy drinking his glass of beer and it was about half full, so I replicated it and poured the beer from the second glass into the real one. They guy kept looking like 'what the heck' but also kept drinking from the glass. I did this about four or five times before he figured out something was going on. He was watching very closely now, so I left. I went up behind Nanny and gave her a kiss on the cheek. She didn't feel it.

I hopped on the last train back home and got in around two in the morning. Since my glasses were glowing I folded them again and it trigged my return to the real world. I was back in the cubby and knew if I tried to get out, Mom would hear me because one of the walls was adjacent to her bedroom. When I heard my dad get up for work, I knew she would think any noise was him, so I opened the door and I got upstairs before he got out of the bathroom.

I went to bed and didn't get up until the following day. Mom thought I was sick, so I didn't have to go to church. Later in the day I was seeing spots before

You're Welcome

my eyes and when I was moving my leg it was clicking and it scared me. I wondered if all this in and out of the altered world was catching up with me.

I told Mom, but she laughed so hard at me I started to cry. Then she tried hard to be serious when she told me that if I stopped looking at the light bulb in the bedroom, the spots would go away. She also said not to crack the joint in my leg anymore and the sound would be gone. Mom was smart, and I always felt better when I talked to her. Both my parents were like that. They always made me feel safe.

The rest of the month was gone before I knew it and we were celebrating Amelia's birthday. Her favorite meal was egg foo young. Mom didn't make it though. It was ordered from a restaurant that Amelia liked. It had to be that restaurant because she said not everyone made it the same.

For birthday dessert we had seven-layer delight which was her favorite. I gave her an extra pinch to grow and inch because even though she was older, I was a few inches taller than her now. After dishes were done I went to visit the girl that had lived next door where the bank is now. Even though she lived in a different city, it was still within walking distance.

Her new house was so much bigger than the old one and after being there several times I knew every inch of it. She liked her new school and had already made many new friends.

I knew it was only a matter of time when our paths would part for good, but I'd always remember her. She said that she had seen her old house by the park and that it was weird seeing other people living there.

Sam and I decided we were going to be airline stewardesses for Halloween this year. Being a Sugar Plum Fairy seemed less grown up. We went up to the thrift store to see if we could find the makings for costumes. We had our pins that we got from the captain of the airplane since they didn't disappear, and they would show up nicely on two crisply ironed white blouses. We found identical dress suits. Both fit.

You're Welcome

They were made of cotton and not quite the right style, but with a little touch up sewing and putting in a small slit up the middle of the back hem, they would do. We needed to find something that would work for the little hats. Mom thought that we could dye a couple of pillbox hats to match. Now that we had that in order we forgot about it again because Halloween was still many weeks off.

We got together to do homework a few times during the weeks that followed. I slept over by her house the Saturday before we went trick or treating. The following weekend would be my birthday and I was going to have a party in the basement. I was excited to be turning thirteen.

I went to church with Sam and stayed to have supper with her family. I made sure I was home in time for Ed Sullivan and ice cream sundaes with the family. I liked that it was something that I could count on. Family was like that. Then it was time to go to bed. Richard and Arthur got up early to use the bathroom.,

Amelia went in next and I was lying in bed thinking. It's hard to believe that it has been almost a year since I turned twelve. In my lifetime I could have never imagined a year like I had or the adventures I had been on.

I still don't know for sure if my older brothers and sister ever had the same adventures or if they remembered them if they did. I wasn't exactly sure why I got to enter the altered realm, but I did know that I had come to understand how important it was to have family. All those many months ago I thought what I truly wanted was to be an only child. I'm thinking now, *'How cool it is that I'm not'*.

Later while I was in the bathroom I heard my younger sister.

"Hey could you hurry up and get out? I need to get in there."

"Sure Helene."

"Thank you." Giggle, Giggle.

You're Welcome

Thank You
Second in the Series SAS
Available Now

By

S. M. Anker

Made in the USA
Monee, IL
28 November 2021

83252387R00194